MICHAEL FRAYN

Noises Off

Michael Frayn has written plays, novels, and screenplays, in addition to being a journalist, documentary filmmaker, and translator of Chekhov. His thirteen plays include *Copenhagen*, which was awarded the Tony Award for Best Play, as well as the Outer Critics Circle and Drama Desk awards and, in the United Kingdom, the Olivier and *Evening Standard* awards. His novel *Headlong* was shortlisted for the Booker Prize. His most recent novel, *Spies*, was published in 2002. Born in London in 1933 and educated at Cambridge, Frayn is married to the biographer and critic Claire Tomalin; they live in London.

Noises Off

A Play in Three Acts

Michael Frayn

Anchor Books
A Division of Random House, Inc.
New York

AN ANCHOR BOOKS ORIGINAL, SEPTEMBER 2002

Copyright © 1982, 1983, and 2000 by Michael Frayn

All rights reserved under International and Pan-American Copyright
Conventions. Published in the United States by Anchor Books, a division of
Random House, Inc., New York, and simultaneously in Canada by Random
House of Canada Limited, Toronto. Originally published in paperback in the
United Kingdom by Methuen Publishing Limited, London, in 2000.

Anchor Books and colophon are registered trademarks of Random House, Inc.

Library of Congress Cataloging-in-Publication Data
Frayn, Michael.
Noises off : a play in three acts / by Michael Frayn.
p.   cm.
ISBN 1-4000-3160-5
1. Theater—Production and direction—Drama.   2. Theatrical companies—
Drama.   3. Actors—Drama.   I. Title.
PR6056.R3 N6 2002
822'.914—dc21
2002071143

www.anchorbooks.com

Printed in the United States of America
10   9   8   7   6   5   4

Author's Note

This play has gone through many different forms and versions. Here, to avoid any mysteries or confusions, is a brief history.

It began life as a short one-actor entitled *Exits,* commissioned by the late Martin Tickner, for a midnight matinee of the Combined Theatrical Charities at the Theatre Royal, Drury Lane, on 10 September 1977, where it was directed by the late Eric Thompson, and played by Denis Quilley, Patricia Routledge, Edward Fox, Dinsdale Landen, and Polly Adams. Michael Codron thereupon commissioned a full-length version, and waited for it with intermittent patience. Michael Blakemore, the director, persuaded me to rethink and restructure for the resulting text, and suggested a great many ideas which I incorporated.

After the play had opened at the Lyric, Hammersmith, in 1982, I did a great deal more rewriting. I went on rewriting, in fact, until Nicky Henson, who was playing Garry, announced on behalf of the cast (rather as Garry himself might have done), that they would learn no further versions.

The play transferred to the Savoy Theatre, and ran until 1987, with five successive casts. For two of the cast-changes I did more rewrites. I also rewrote for the production in Washington in 1983, and I rewrote again when this moved to Broadway.

Reading the English text that has been in use in the past decade and a half I have discovered a series of bizarre misprints, and I suspect that directors have been driven to some quite outlandish devices to make sense of them. What's happened to it in other languages I can for the most part only guess. I know that in France it has been played under two different titles (sometimes simultaneously), and in Germany under four. I imagine that it's often been freely adapted to local circumstances, in spite of the prohibitions in the contract. In France, certainly, my British actors and the characters they are playing turned into Frenchmen, in Italy into Italians (who introduced a 'Sardine Song' between the acts). In Barcelona they were Catalan-speaking actors playing Spanish-speaking characters; in Tampere, in northern Finland, they were robust northerners speaking the Tampere dialect and playing effete southerners with Helsinki accents. On the Japanese poster they all appear to be Japanese; on the Chinese poster Chinese. In Prague they performed the play for some ten years without Act Three, and no one noticed until I arrived.

For the revival at the National Theatre in 2000 I've rewritten yet again. Some of the changes are ones that I've been longing to make myself – there's nothing like having to sit through a play twelve million times to make your fingers itch for the delete key. Many other changes were suggested by the radical criticisms and irresistible inventions of my new director, Jeremy Sams. I hope that no one will consciously notice the difference, but if I have demolished any particularly cherished errors or suggestive inconsistencies I apologise.

Publisher's Note

Noises Off was first presented, by arrangement with Michael Codron, at the Lyric Theatre, Hammersmith, on 23 February 1982, and on 31 March by Michael Codron at the Savoy Theatre, London, with the following cast:

Dotty Otley	Patricia Routledge
Lloyd Dallas	Paul Eddington
Garry Lejeune	Nicky Henson
Brooke Ashton	Rowena Roberts
Poppy Norton-Taylor	Yvonne Antrobus
Frederick Fellowes	Tony Matthews
Belinda Blair	Jan Waters
Tim Allgood	Roger Lloyd Pack
Selsdon Mowbray	Michael Aldridge
Electrician	Ray Edwards

Directed by Michael Blakemore
Designed by Michael Annals
Lighting by Spike Gaden

It was revived in its present form by the Royal National Theatre, in association with the Ambassador Theatre Group and Act Productions Ltd. It previewed in the Lyttelton Theatre on 29 September 2000, and opened on 5 October, with the following cast:

Dotty Otley	Patricia Hodge
Lloyd Dallas	Peter Egan
Garry Lejeune	Aden Gillett
Brooke Ashton	Natalie Walter
Poppy Norton-Taylor	Selina Griffiths
Frederick Fellowes	Jeff Rawle
Belinda Blair	Susie Blake
Tim Allgood	Paul Thornley
Selsdon Mowbray	Christopher Benjamin

Directed by Jeremy Sams
Designed by Robert Jones
Lighting by Tim Mitchell
Sound by Fergus O'Hare for Aura

On 14 May 2001 this production opened at the Piccadilly Theatre, London, with the same cast except for:

Dotty Otley	Lynn Redgrave
Garry Lejeune	Stephen Mangan

It opened at the Brooks Atkinson Theatre, New York, on 1 November 2001, with the following cast:

Dotty Otley	Patti LuPone
Lloyd Dallas	Peter Gallagher
Garry Lejeune	Thomas McCarthy
Brooke Ashton	Katie Finneran
Poppy Norton-Taylor	Robin Weigert
Frederick Fellowes	Faith Prince
Belinda Blair	Edward Hibbert
Tim Allgood	T. R. Knight
Selsdon Mowbray	Richard Easton

Directed by Jeremy Sams
Designed by Robert Jones
Lighting by Tim Mitchell
Sound by Fergus O'Hare for Aura

The cast of *Noises Off* are performing another play, *Nothing On.* The casting in *Nothing On* is as follows:

Mrs. Clackett	Dotty Otley
Roger Tramplemain	Garry Lejeune
Vicki	Brooke Ashton
Philip Brent	Frederick Fellowes
Flavia Brent	Belinda Blair
Burglar	Selsdon Mowbray
Sheikh	Frederick Fellowes

Director Lloyd Dallas
Company and Stage Manager Tim Allgood
Assistant Stage Manager Poppy Norton-Taylor

Noises Off

The action takes place in the living-room of the Brents' country home, on a Wednesday afternoon.

Act One: *The living-room of the Brents' country home. Wednesday afternoon.*
(Grand Theatre, Weston-super-Mare. Monday 14 January)

Act One: *The living-room of the Brents' country home. Wednesday afternoon.*
(Theatre Royal, Ashton-under-Lyne. Wednesday matinee, 13 February)

Act One: *The living-room of the Brents' country home. Wednesday afternoon.*
(Municipal Theatre, Stockton-on-Tees. Saturday 6 April)

There is an interval between Act One and Act One. There is no interval between Act One and Act One.

Act One

The living-room of the Brents' country home. Wednesday afternoon.

(Grand Theatre, Weston-super-Mare. Monday 14 January.)

From the estate agent's description of the property:

A delightful 16th-century posset mill, 25 miles from London. Lovingly converted, old-world atmosphere, many period features. Fully equipped with every aid to modern living and beautifully furnished throughout by owner now resident abroad. Ideal for overseas company seeking perfect English setting to house senior executive. Minimum three months' let. Apply sole agents: Squire, Squire, Hackham and Dudley.

The accommodation comprises: an open-plan living area, with a staircase leading to a gallery. A notable feature is the extensive range of entrances and exits provided. On the ground floor the front door gives access to the mature garden and delightful village beyond. Another door leads to the elegant panelled study, and a third to the light and airy modern service quarters. A fourth door opens into a luxurious bathroom/WC suite, and a full-length south-facing window affords extensive views. On the gallery level is the door to the master bedroom, and another to a small but well-proportioned linen cupboard. A corridor gives access to all the other rooms in the upper parts of the house. Another beautifully equipped bathroom/WC suite opens off the landing halfway up the stairs.

All in all, a superb example of the traditional English set-builder's craft – a place where the discerning theatregoer will feel instantly at home.

Introductory music. As the curtain rises, the award-winning modern telephone is ringing.

Enter from the service quarters **Mrs Clackett***, a housekeeper of character. She is carrying an imposing plate of sardines.*

Mrs Clackett   It's no good you going on. I can't open sardines *and* answer the phone. I've only got one pair of feet.

She puts the sardines down on the telephone table by the sofa, and picks up the phone.

Hello . . . Yes, but there's no one here, love . . . No, Mr Brent's not here . . . He lives here, yes, but he don't live here now because he lives in Spain . . . Mr Philip Brent, that's right . . . The one who writes the plays, that's him, only now he writes them in Spain . . . No, she's in Spain, too, they're all in Spain, there's no one here . . . Am *I* in Spain? No, I'm not in Spain, dear. I look after the house for them, but I go home at one o'clock on Wednesday, only I've got a nice plate of sardines to put my feet up with, because it's the royal what's it called on the telly – the royal you know – where's the paper, then . . .?

She picks up the newspaper lying on the sofa and searches in it.

. . . And if it's to do with letting the house then you'll have to ring the house agents, because they're the agents for the house . . . Squire, Squire, Hackham and who's the other one . . .? No, they're not in Spain, they're next to the phone in the study. Squire, Squire, Hackham, and hold on, I'll go and look.

She replaces the receiver.

Or so the stage-directions say in Robin Housemonger's play, Nothing On. *In fact, though, she puts the receiver down beside the phone instead.*

Always the same, isn't it. Soon as you take the weight off your feet, down it all comes on your head.

Exit **Mrs Clackett** *into the study, still holding the newspaper.*

Or so the stage direction says. In fact, she moves off holding the plate of sardines instead of the newspaper. As she does so, **Dotty Otley**, *the actress who is playing the part of* **Mrs Clackett**, *comes out of character to comment on the move.*

Dotty   And l take the sardines. No, I leave the sardines. No, I take the sardines.

The disembodied voice of **Lloyd Dallas**, *the director of* Nothing On, *replies from somewhere out in the darkness of the auditorium.*

Lloyd   You leave the sardines and you put the receiver back.

Dotty   Oh yes, I put the receiver back.

She puts the receiver back and moves off again with the sardines.

Lloyd   And you leave the sardines.

Dotty   And I *leave* the sardines?

Lloyd   You *leave* the sardines.

Dotty   I put the receiver back and I leave the sardines.

Lloyd   Right.

Dotty   We've changed that, have we, love?

Lloyd   No, love.

Dotty   That's what I've always been doing?

Lloyd   I shouldn't say that, Dotty, my precious.

Dotty   How about the words, love? Am I getting some of them right?

Lloyd   Some of them have a very familiar ring.

Dotty   Only it's like a fruit machine in there.

Lloyd   I know that, Dotty.

Dotty   I open my mouth, and I never know if it's going to come out three oranges or two lemons and a banana.

Lloyd   Anyway, it's not midnight yet. We don't open till tomorrow. So you're holding the receiver.

Dotty   I'm holding the receiver.

Lloyd   'Squire, Squire, Hackham and, hold on . . .'

Dotty *resumes her performance as* **Mrs Clackett**.

Mrs Clackett   Squire, Squire, Hackham and, hold on, don't go away, I'm putting it down.

She replaces the receiver.

Always the same, isn't it. Put your feet up for two minutes and immediately they come running after you.

Exit **Mrs Clackett** *into the study, still holding the newspaper.*

Only she isn't holding the newspaper.

The sound of a key in the lock.

Lloyd   Hold it.

The front door opens. On the doorstep stands **Roger**, *holding a cardboard box. He is about thirty and has the well-appointed air of a man who handles high-class real estate.*

Roger   . . . I have a housekeeper, yes, but this is her afternoon off.

Lloyd   Hold it, Garry. Dotty!

Enter **Vicki** *through the front door. She is a desirable property in her early twenties, well-built and beautifully maintained throughout.*

Roger   So we've got the place entirely to ourselves.

Lloyd   Hold it, Brooke. Dotty!

Enter **Dotty** *from the study.*

Dotty   Come back?

Lloyd   Yes, and go out again with the *newspaper*.

Dotty   The newspaper? Oh, the newspaper.

Lloyd   You put the receiver back, you leave the sardines and you go out with the newspaper.

Garry   Here you are, love.

Dotty   Sorry, love.

Garry (*embraces her*)   Don't worry, love. It's only the technical.

Lloyd   It's the dress, Garry, honey. It's the dress rehearsal.

Garry   So when was the technical?

Lloyd   So when's the dress? We open tomorrow!

Garry   Well, we're all thinking of it as the technical. (*To* **Dotty**.) Aren't we, love?

Dotty   It's all those words, my sweetheart.

Garry   Don't worry about the words, Dotty, my pet.

Dotty   Coming up like oranges and lemons.

Garry   Listen, Dotty, your words are fine, your words are better than the, do you know what I mean? (*To* **Brooke**.) Isn't that right?

Brooke (*her thoughts elsewhere*)   Sorry?

Garry (*to* **Dotty**)   I mean, OK, so he's the, you know. Fine. But, Dotty, love, you've been playing this kind of part for, well, you know what I mean.

Lloyd   All right? So Garry and Brooke are off, Dotty's holding the receiver . . .

Garry   No, but here we are, we're all thinking, my God, we open tomorrow, we've only had a fortnight to rehearse, we don't know where we are, but my God, here we are!

Dotty   That's right, my sweet. Isn't that right, Lloyd?

Lloyd   Beautifully put, Garry.

Garry   No, but we've got to play Weston-super-Mare all the rest of this week, then Yeovil, then God knows where, then God knows where else, and so on for God knows how long, and we're all of us feeling pretty much, you know . . . (*To* **Brooke**.) I mean, aren't *you*?

Brooke   Sorry?

Lloyd   Anyway, you're off, Dotty's holding the receiver . . .

Garry   Sorry, Lloyd. But sometimes you just have to come right out with it. You know?

Lloyd   I know.

Garry   Thanks, Lloyd.

Lloyd   OK, Garry. So you're off . . .

Garry   Lloyd, let me just say one thing. Since we've stopped. I've worked with a lot of directors, Lloyd. Some of them were geniuses. Some of them were bastards. But I've never met one who was so totally and absolutely . . . I don't know . . .

Lloyd   Thank you, Garry. I'm very touched. Now will you get off the fucking stage?

Exit **Garry** *through the front door.*

Lloyd   And, Brooke . . .

Brooke   Yes?

Lloyd   Are you in?

Brooke   In?

Lloyd   Are you there?

Brooke   What?

Lloyd   You're out. OK. I'll call again. And on we go.

Exit **Brooke** *through the front door.*

Lloyd   So there you are, holding the receiver.

Dotty   So there I am, holding the receiver. I put the receiver back and I leave the sardines.

Mrs Clackett   Always the same story, isn't it . . .

Lloyd   And you take the newspaper.

She comes back, and picks up the newspaper and the receiver.

Dotty   I leave the sardines, I take the newspaper.

Mrs Clackett   Always the same story, isn't it. It's a weight off your mind, it's a load off your stomach.

Dotty   And off at last I go.

Lloyd   Leaving the receiver.

She replaces the receiver and goes off into the study. Enter **Roger** *as before, with the cardboard box.*

Roger   . . . I have a housekeeper, yes, but this is her afternoon off.

Enter **Vicki** *as before.*

Roger   So we've got the place entirely to ourselves.

Roger *goes back and brings in a flight bag, and closes the front door.*

I'll just check.

He opens the door to the service quarters. **Vicki** *gazes round.*

Roger   Hello? Anyone at home?

Closes the door.

No, there's no one here. So what do you think?

Vicki   Great. And this is all yours?

Roger   Just a little shack in the woods, really. Converted posset mill. Sixteenth-century.

Vicki   It must have cost a bomb.

Roger   Well, one has to have somewhere to entertain one's business associates. Someone coming at four o'clock, in fact. Arab sheikh. Oil. You know.

Vicki   Right. And I've got to get those files to our Basingstoke office by four.

Roger   Yes, we'll only just manage to fit it in. I mean, we'll only just do it. I mean . . .

Vicki   Right, then.

Roger   (*putting down the box and opening the flight bag*)   We won't bother to chill the champagne.

Vicki   All these doors!

Roger   Oh, only a handful, really. (*He opens the various doors one after another to demonstrate.*) Study. . . Kitchen . . . And a self-contained service flat for the housekeeper.

Vicki   Terrific. And which one's the . . . ?

Roger   What?

Vicki   You know . . .

Roger   The usual offices? Through here. (*He opens the downstairs bathroom door for her.*)

Vicki   Fantastic.

Exit **Vicki** *into the bathroom.*

Enter **Mrs Clackett** *from the study, without the newspaper.*

Mrs Clackett   Now I've lost the sardines . . .

Mutual surprise. **Roger** *closes the door to the bathroom and slips the champagne back into the bag.*

Roger   I'm sorry. I thought there was no one here.

Mrs Clackett   I'm not here. I'm off, only it's the royal you know, where they wear those hats, and they're all covered in fruit, and who are you?

Roger   I'm from the agents.

Mrs Clackett   From the agents?

Roger   Squire, Squire, Hackham and Dudley.

Mrs Clackett   Oh. Which one are you, then? Squire, Squire, Hackham, or Dudley?

Roger   I'm Tramplemain.

Mrs Clackett   Walking in here as if you owned the place! I thought you was a burglar.

Roger   No, I just dropped in to . . . go into a few things . . .

The bathroom door opens. **Roger** *closes it.*

Well, to check some of the measurements . . .

The bathroom door opens. **Roger** *closes it.*

Do one or two odd jobs . . .

The bathroom door opens. **Roger** *closes it.*

Oh, and a client. I'm showing a prospective tenant over the house.

The bathroom door opens.

Vicki   What's wrong with this door?

Roger *closes it.*

Roger   She's thinking of renting it. Her interest is definitely aroused.

Enter **Vicki** *from bathroom.*

Vicki   That's not the bedroom.

Roger   The bedroom? No, that's the downstairs bathroom and WC suite. And this is the housekeeper, Mrs Crockett.

Mrs Clackett   Clackett, dear, Clackett.

Vicki   Oh. Hi.

Roger   She's not really here.

Mrs Clackett   Only it's the royal, you know, with the hats.

Roger (*to* **Mrs Clackett**)   Don't worry about us.

Mrs Clackett (*picks up the sardines*)   I'll have the sound on low.

Roger   We'll just inspect the house.

Mrs Clackett   Only now I've lost the newspaper.

Exit **Mrs Clackett** *into the study, carrying the sardines.*

Only she leaves them behind.

Lloyd   Sardines!

Roger   I'm sorry about this.

Vicki   That's all right. We don't want the television, do we?

Lloyd   Sardines!

Enter **Dotty** *from the study.*

Dotty   I've forgotten the sardines.

Garry   Lloyd! These sardines! They're driving us all mad!

Lloyd   Something wrong with the sardines? Poppy!

Garry   There's four plates of sardines coming on in Act One alone! They go here, they go there. *She* takes them – *I* take them. (*To* **Brooke**.) I mean, don't *you* feel, you know?

Brooke (*elsewhere again*)   Sorry?

Garry   The sardines.

Brooke   What sardines?

Enter **Poppy**, *the assistant stage manager, from the wings.*

Poppy   Change the sardines?

Lloyd   Make it four grilled turbot. Off the bone.

Garry (*to* **Lloyd**)   OK, it's all right for you. You're sitting out there. We're up here. We've got to *do* it. Plus we've got bags, we've got boxes. Plus doors. Plus words. You know what I mean?

Dotty   We're not getting at you, Poppy, love. We think the sardines are lovely.

Garry   I'm just trying to, you know.

Lloyd   So what *do* you want to change, Garry? The bags?
The boxes? The doors?

Dotty   We can't start *changing* things now, love!

Garry   I'm just *saying*. Words. Doors. Bags. Boxes.
Sardines. *Us*. OK? I've made my point?

Lloyd   You certainly have, Garry. Got that, Poppy?

Poppy   Um. Well.

Lloyd   Right. On we go. From Dotty's exit. And Poppy . . .

Poppy   Yes?

Lloyd   Don't let this happen again.

Poppy   Oh. No.

Exit **Poppy** *into the wings.*

Garry   Sorry, Lloyd. I just thought we ought to, do you
know what I mean?

Lloyd   Of course.

Garry   Better out than, you know.

Lloyd   Much better. As long as Dotty's happy.

Dotty   Absolutely happy, Lloyd, my love.

She goes to the study door.

Lloyd   Will you do something for me then, Dotty, my
precious?

Dotty   Anything, Lloyd, my sweet.

Lloyd   Take the sardines off with you.

Exit **Mrs Clackett** *into study, carrying the sardines.*

Roger   I'm sorry about this.

Vicki   That's all right. We don't want the television, do
we?

Roger   Only she's been in the family for generations.

Vicki   Great. Come on, then. (*She starts upstairs.*) I've got to be in Basingstoke by four.

Roger   Perhaps we should just have a glass of champagne.

Vicki   We'll take it up with us.

Roger   Yes. Well . . .

Vicki   And don't let my files out of sight.

Roger   No. Only . . .

Vicki   What?

Roger   Well . . .

Vicki   Her?

Roger   She *has* been in the family for generations.

Enter **Mrs Clackett** *from the study, with the newspaper but without the sardines.*

Mrs Clackett   Sardines . . . Sardines . . . It's not for me to say, of course, dear, only I will just say this: don't think twice about it – take the plunge. You'll really enjoy it here.

Vicki   Oh. Great.

Mrs Clackett (*to* **Roger**)   Won't she, love?

Roger   Yes. Well. Yes!

Mrs Clackett (*to* **Vicki**)   And we'll enjoy having you. (*To* **Roger**.) Won't we, love?

Roger   Oh. Well.

Vicki   Terrific.

Mrs Clackett   Sardines, sardines. Can't put your feet up on an empty stomach, can you.

Exit **Mrs Clackett** *to service quarters.*

Vicki   You see? She thinks it's great. She's even making us sardines!

Roger   Well . . .

Vicki   I think she's terrific.

Roger   Terrific.

Vicki   So which way?

Roger (*picking up the bags*)   All right. Before she comes back with the sardines.

Vicki   Up here?

Roger   Yes, yes.

Vicki   In here?

Roger   Yes, yes, yes.

Exeunt **Roger** *and* **Vicki** *into mezzanine bathroom.*

Vicki (*off*)   It's another bathroom.

They reappear.

Roger   No, no, no.

Vicki   Always trying to get me into bathrooms.

Roger   I mean in *here.*

He nods at the next door – the first along the gallery. **Vicki** *leads the way in.* **Roger** *follows.*

Vicki   Oh, black sheets! (*She produces one.*)

Roger   It's the airing cupboard. (*He throws the sheet back.*) This one, this one.

He drops the bag and box, and struggles nervously to open the second door along the gallery, the bedroom.

Vicki   Oh, you're in a real state! You can't even get the door open.

Exeunt **Roger** *and* **Vicki** *into the bedroom.*

Only they can't, because the bedroom door won't open.

> *The sound of a key in the lock, and the front door opens. On the doorstep stands **Philip**, carrying a cardboard box. He is in his forties, with a deep suntan, and writes attractive new plays with a charming period atmosphere.*
>
> **Philip**   . . . No, it's Mrs Clackett's afternoon off, remember.

Lloyd   Hold it.

> *Enter **Flavia**, carrying a flight bag like **Roger**'s. She is in her thirties, the perfect companion piece to the above.*

Lloyd   Hold it.

> **Philip**   We've got the place entirely to ourselves.
>
> **Philip** *closes the door.*

*Only the door won't stay closed. A pause, while **Garry** struggles to open the door upstairs, and **Frederick** struggles to close the door downstairs.*

Lloyd   And God said, Hold it. And they held it. And God saw that it was terrible.

Garry (*to **Frederick** and **Belinda**, the actor and actress playing **Philip** and **Flavia***)   Sorry, loves, this door won't open.

Belinda   Sorry, love, this door won't close.

Lloyd   And God said, 'Poppy!'

Frederick   Sorry, everyone. Am I doing something wrong? You know how stupid I am about doors.

Belinda   Freddie, my sweet, you're doing it perfectly.

Frederick   As long as it's not me that's broken it.

*Enter **Poppy** from the wings.*

Lloyd   And there was Poppy. And God said, Be fruitful and multiply, and fetch Tim to fix the doors.

Exit **Poppy** *into the wings.*

Belinda   Oh, I love technicals!

Garry   She loves technicals! (*Fondly.*) Isn't she just, I mean, honestly, she loves technicals! Dotty! Where's Dotty?

Belinda   Everyone's always so nice to everyone.

Garry   Oh! Isn't she just, I mean, she really is, isn't she.

Enter **Dotty** *from the service quarters.*

Garry (*to* **Dotty**)   Belinda's being all, you know.

Belinda   But Freddie, my precious, don't *you* like a nice all-night technical?

Frederick   The only thing I like about technicals is you get a chance to sit on the furniture. (*He sits.*)

Belinda   Oh, Freddie, my precious! It's lovely to see you cheering up and making jokes.

She sits beside him and embraces him.

Frederick   Oh, was that a joke?

Belinda   This is such a lovely company to work with. It's such a happy company.

Dotty   Wait till we've got to Stockton-on-Tees in twelve weeks time.

Belinda (*sits*)   Are you all right, Lloyd, my precious?

Lloyd   I'm starting to know what God felt like when he sat out there in the darkness creating the world. (*He takes a pill.*)

Belinda   What did he feel like, Lloyd, my love?

Lloyd   Very pleased he'd taken his Valium.

Belinda   He had six days, of course. We've only got six hours.

Lloyd   And God said, 'Where the fuck is Tim?'

Enter from the wings **Tim**, *the company stage manager. He is exhausted.*

Lloyd   And there the fuck *was* Tim. And God said, 'Let there be doors, that open when they open, and close when they close.'

Tim   Do something?

Lloyd   Doors.

Tim   I was doing the front of house.

Lloyd   Doors.

Tim   Doors?

Lloyd   Tim, are you fully awake?

Belinda   Lloyd, he *has* been putting the set up all weekend.

Lloyd   You're not trying to do too much, are you, Tim?

Belinda   Tim, my love, this door won't close.

Garry   And the bedroom won't, you know.

Tim   Oh, right. (*He sets to work on the doors.*)

Belinda (*to* **Lloyd**)   He hasn't been to bed for forty-eight hours.

Lloyd   Don't worry, Tim. Only another twenty-four hours, and it'll be the end of the day.

Lloyd *comes up on stage.*

Belinda   Oh, look, he's come down to earth amongst us.

Lloyd   Listen. Since we've stopped anyway. OK, it took two days to get the set up, so we shan't have time for a dress rehearsal. Don't worry. Think of the first night as a dress rehearsal. If we can just get through the play once tonight for doors and sardines. That's what it's all about. Doors and sardines. Getting on – getting off. Getting the sardines on –

getting the sardines off. That's farce. That's the theatre. That's life.

Belinda   Oh, Lloyd, you're so deep.

Lloyd   So just keep going. Bang, bang, bang. Bang you're on. Bang you've said it. Bang you're off. And everything will be perfectly . . . where's Selsdon?

Belinda   Oh no!

Garry   Not already?

Belinda   Selsdon!

Garry   Selsdon!

Lloyd   Poppy!

Dotty (*to* **Lloyd**)   I thought he was in front, with you?

Lloyd   I thought he was round the back, with you?

Enter **Poppy** *from the wings.*

Lloyd   Is Mr Mowbray in his dressing-room?

Exit **Poppy** *into the wings.*

Frederick   Oh, I don't think he would. Not at a technical. (*To* **Brooke**.) Would he?

Brooke   Would who?

Garry   Selsdon. We can't find him!

Frederick   I'm sure he wouldn't. Not at a technical.

Dotty   Half a chance, he would.

Brooke   Would what?

Garry, **Dotty** *and* **Lloyd** *make gestures to her of tipping a glass, or raising the elbow, or screwing the nose.*

Belinda   Now come on, my sweets, be fair! We don't know.

Frederick   Let's not jump to any conclusions.

Lloyd   Let's just get the understudy dressed. Tim!

Tim   Yes?

Lloyd   Hurry up with those doors. You're going on as the Burglar.

Tim   Oh. Right.

Dotty   He shouldn't have been out of sight! I said, he must never be out of sight!

Belinda   He's been as good as gold all the way through rehearsals.

Garry   Yes, because in the rehearsal room it was all, I don't know, but there we were, do you know what I mean?

Lloyd   There was no set. You could see everyone.

Garry   And here it's all, you know.

Lloyd   Split into two. There's a front and a back. And instantly we've lost him.

Enter **Poppy** *from the wings.*

Poppy   He's not in the dressing-room.

Dotty   You've looked in the lavatories?

Poppy   Yes.

Dotty   And the scenery dock and the prop room and the paint store?

Poppy   Yes.

Frederick (*to* **Dotty**)   You've worked with him before, of course.

Lloyd (*to* **Poppy**)   Ring the police.

Exit **Poppy** *into the wings.*

Lloyd (*to* **Tim**)   Finished the doors? Right, get the Burglar gear on.

Exit **Tim** *into the wings.*

Enter **Selsdon Mowbray** *from the back of the stalls. He is in his seventies and is wearing his* **Burglar** *gear. He comes down the aisle during the following dialogue and stands in front of the stage, watching everyone on it.*

Lloyd   I'm sorry, Dotty, my love.

Dotty   No, it's my fault, Lloyd, my love.

Lloyd   I cast him.

Dotty   'Let's give him one last chance,' I said. 'One last chance!' I mean, what can you do? We were in weekly rep together in Peebles.

Garry (*to* **Dotty**)   It's my fault, my precious. I shouldn't have let you. This tour for her isn't just, do you know what I mean? This is her life savings!

Lloyd   We know that, Garry, love.

Belinda *puts a hand on* **Dotty**'*s arm.*

Dotty   I'm not trying to make my fortune.

Frederick   Of course you're not, Dotty.

Dotty   I just wanted to put a little something by.

Belinda   We know, love.

Garry   Just something to buy a little house that she could, I mean, come on, that's not so much to ask.

Brooke *puts a hand to her eye.*

Belinda (*to* **Brooke**)   Don't *you* cry, my sweet! It's not *your* fault!

Brook   No, I've got something behind my lens.

Frederick   Yes, you couldn't expect Brooke to keep anyone in sight.

Dotty (*pointing at* **Selsdon** *without seeing him*)   But he was standing right there in the stalls before we started! I saw him!

Brooke   Who are we talking about now?

Belinda   It's all right, my sweet. We know you can't see anything.

Brooke   You mean *Selsdon*? I'm not *blind*. I can see *Selsdon*.

They all turn and see him.

Belinda   Selsdon!

Garry   Oh my God, he's here all the time!

Lloyd   Standing there like Hamlet's father.

Frederick   My word, Selsdon, you gave us a surprise. We thought you were . . . We thought you were . . . not there.

Dotty   Where have you been, Selsdon?

Belinda   Are you all right, Selsdon?

Lloyd   Speak to us!

Selsdon   Is it a party?

Belinda   'Is it a party?'!

Selsdon   Is it? How killing! I got it into my head there was going to be a rehearsal. (*He goes up on to the stage.*) I was having a little postprandial snooze at the back of the stalls so as to be ready for the rehearsal.

Belinda   Isn't he lovely?

Lloyd   Much lovelier now we can see him.

Selsdon   So what are we celebrating?

Belinda   'What are we celebrating?'!

Enter **Tim** *from the wings.*

Tim   I've looked all through his dressing-room. I've looked all through the wardrobe. I can't find the gear.

Lloyd *indicates* **Selsdon**

Tim   Oh.

Selsdon   Beer? In the wardrobe?

Lloyd   No, Selsdon. Tim, you need a break. Why don't you sit down quietly upstairs and do all the company's VAT?

Tim   VAT, right.

Lloyd (*discreetly*)   And Tim – just in case he and the gear *do* walk off together one night, order yourself a spare Burglar costume.

Tim   Spare Burglar costume.

Lloyd   *Two* spare Burglar costumes. One to fit you, one to fit Poppy. I want a plentiful supply of spare Burglars on hand for any eventuality.

Tim   Two spare Burglars.

Exit **Tim** *into the wings.*

Belinda   He has been on his feet for forty-eight hours, Lloyd.

Lloyd (*calling*)   Don't fall down, Tim. We may not be insured.

Selsdon   So what's next on the bill?

Lloyd   Well, Selsdon, I thought we might try a spot of rehearsal.

Selsdon   Oh, I won't, thank you.

Lloyd   You *won't?*

Selsdon   You all go ahead. I'll sit and watch you. This is the beer in the wardrobe, is it?

Belinda   No, my sweet, he wants us to rehearse.

Selsdon   Yes, but I think we've got to rehearse, haven't we?

Lloyd   Rehearse, yes! Well done, Selsdon. I knew you'd think of something. Right, from Belinda and Freddie's entrance . . .

Enter **Poppy** *from the wings, alarmed.*

Poppy   Lloyd . . .

Lloyd   What? What's happened now?

Poppy   The police!

Lloyd   The *police*?

Poppy   They've found an old man. He was lying unconscious in a doorway just across the street.

Lloyd   Oh. Yes. Thank you.

Poppy   They say he's very dirty and rather smelly, and I thought oh my God, because . . .

Lloyd   Thank you, Poppy.

Poppy   Because when you get close to Selsdon . . .

Belinda   Poppy!

Poppy   No, I mean, if you stand anywhere near Selsdon you can't help noticing this very distinctive. . . (*She stops, sniffing.*)

Selsdon (*putting his arm round her*)   I'll tell you something, Poppy. Once you've got it in your nostrils you never forget it. Sixty years now and the smell of the theatre still haunts me.

Exit **Selsdon** *into the study.*

Belinda   Oh, bless him!

Lloyd   Tell me, Poppy, love – how did you get a job like this, that requires tact and understanding? You're not somebody's girlfriend, are you?

Poppy *gives him a startled look.*

Belinda   Don't worry, Poppy, my sweet. He truly did not hear.

Enter **Selsdon** *from the study.*

Selsdon   *Not* here?

Lloyd   Yes, yes, there!

Belinda   Sit down, my precious.

Dotty   Go back to sleep.

Lloyd   You're not on for another twenty pages yet.

Exit **Selsdon** *into the study. Exit* **Poppy** *into the wings.*

Lloyd   And on we go.

He goes back down into the auditorium.

Dotty in the kitchen, wildly roasting sardines. Freddie and Belinda waiting impatiently outside the front door. Garry and Brooke disappearing tremulously into the bedroom. Time sliding irrevocably into the past.

Exeunt **Dotty** *into the service quarters,* **Garry** *and* **Brooke** *upstairs into the bedroom, and* **Frederick** *through the front door.*

Belinda (*to* **Lloyd**, *with lowered voice*)   Aren't they sweet?

Lloyd   What?

Belinda (*points to the bedroom and the service quarters*)   Garry and Dotty.

Lloyd   Garry and Dotty?

Belinda   Sh!

Lloyd (*lowers his voice*)   What? You mean they're an item? Those two? Tramplemain and Mrs Clackett?

Belinda   It's supposed to be a secret.

Lloyd   But she's old enough to be . . .

Belinda   Sh! Didn't you know?

Lloyd   I'm just God, Belinda, love. I'm just the one with the English degree, I don't know anything.

Enter **Garry** *from the bedroom.*

Garry   What's happening?

Lloyd   I don't like to imagine, Garry, honey.

Exit **Belinda** *through the front door.*

Garry   I mean, what are we waiting for?

Enter **Dotty** *from the service quarters, inquiringly.*

Lloyd   I don't know what you're waiting for, Garry. Her sixteenth birthday?

Garry   What?

Lloyd   Or maybe just the cue. Brooke!

Exit **Dotty** *to the service quarters.*

Enter **Brooke** *from the bedroom.*

Lloyd   'Oh, you're in a real state.'

> **Vicki**   Oh, you're in a real state! You can't even get the door open.

Lloyd   Door closed, love.

Garry *closes the door.*

> **Vicki**   You can't even get the door open.
>
> *Exeunt* **Roger** *and* **Vicki** *into the bedroom.*
>
> *Enter* **Philip** *through the front door.*

Philip No, it's Mrs Clackett's afternoon off, remember.

Enter **Flavia**, *carrying a flight bag like* **Roger**'s.

Philip We've got the place entirely to ourselves.

Philip *closes the door.*

Flavia Home!

Philip Home, sweet home!

Flavia Dear old house!

Philip Just waiting for us to come back!

Flavia It's rather funny, though, creeping in like this for our wedding anniversary!

Philip It's damned serious! If Inland Revenue find out we're in the country, even for one night, bang goes our claim to be resident abroad. Bang goes most of this year's income. I feel like an illegal immigrant.

Flavia I'll tell you what I feel like.

Philip Champagne? (*He takes a bottle out of the box.*)

Flavia I wonder if Mrs Clackett's aired the beds.

Philip Darling!

Flavia Well, why not? No children. No friends dropping in. We're absolutely on our own.

Philip True. (*He picks up the bag and box, and ushers* **Flavia** *towards the stairs.*) There is something to be said for being a tax exile.

Flavia Leave those!

He drops the bag and box, and kisses her. She flees upstairs, laughing, and he after her.

Philip Sh!

Flavia What?

Philip (*humorously*)   Inland Revenue may hear us!

They creep to the bedroom door.

Enter **Mrs Clackett** *from the service quarters, carrying a fresh plate of sardines.*

Mrs Clackett (*to herself*)   What I did with that first lot of sardines I shall never know.

She puts the sardines on the telephone table and sits on the sofa.

Philip *and* **Flavia** (*looking down from the gallery*)   Mrs Clackett!

Mrs Clackett *jumps up.*

Mrs Clackett   Oh, you give me a turn! My heart jumped right out of my boots!

Philip   So did mine!

Flavia   We thought you'd gone!

Mrs Clackett   I thought you was in Spain!

Philip   We are! We are!

Flavia   You haven't seen us!

Philip   We're not here!

Mrs Clackett   Oh, like that, is it? The income tax are after you?

Flavia   They would be, if they knew we were here.

Mrs Clackett   All right, then, love. You're not here. I haven't seen you. Anybody asks for you, I don't know nothing. Off to bed, are you?

Philip   Oh . . .

Flavia   Well . . .

Mrs Clackett   That's right. Nowhere like bed when they all get on top of you. You'll want your things, look. (*She indicates the bag and box.*)

Philip   Oh. Yes. Thanks.

He comes downstairs, and picks up the bag and box.

Mrs Clackett (*to* **Flavia**)   Oh, and that bed hasn't been aired, love.

Flavia   I'll get a hot-water bottle.

Exit **Flavia** *into the mezzanine bathroom.*

Mrs Clackett   I've put all your letters in the study, dear.

Philip   Letters? What letters? You forward all the mail, don't you?

Mrs Clackett   Not the ones from the income tax, dear. I don't want to spoil your holidays.

Philip   Oh, good heavens! Where are they?

Mrs Clackett   I've put them all in the pigeonhouse.

Philip   In the *pigeonhouse*?

Mrs Clackett   In the little pigeonhouse in your desk, love.

Exeunt **Mrs Clackett** *and* **Philip** *into the study.* **Philip** *is still holding the bag and box.*

Only he remains on and **Dotty** *remains in the doorway waiting for him.*

Enter **Roger** *from the bedroom, still dressed, tying his tie.*

Roger   Yes, but I could hear voices!

Enter **Vicki** *from the bedroom in her underwear.*

Vicki   Voices? What sort of voices?

Lloyd   Hold it. Freddie, what's the trouble?

Frederick   Lloyd, you know how stupid I am about moves. Sorry, Garry . . . Sorry, Brooke . . . It's just my usual dimness. (*To* **Lloyd**.) But why do I take the things off into the study? Wouldn't it be more natural if I left them on?

Lloyd   No.

Frederick   I thought it might be somehow more logical.

Lloyd   No.

Frederick   Lloyd, I know it's a bit late in the day to go into all this. . .

Lloyd   Freddie, we've got several more minutes left before we open.

Enter **Belinda** *from the mezzanine bathroom, to wait patiently.*

Frederick   Thank you, Lloyd. As long as we're not too pushed. But I've never understood why he carries an overnight bag and a box of groceries into the study to look at his mail.

Garry   Because they have to be out of the way for my next scene!

Frederick   I see that.

Belinda   And Freddie, my sweet, Selsdon needs them in the study for *his* scene.

Frederick   I see that . . .

Lloyd (*comes up on stage*)   Selsdon . . . where is he? Is he there?

Belinda (*calling, urgently*)   Selsdon!

Dotty (*likewise*)   Selsdon!

Garry (*likewise*)   Selsdon!

A pane of glass shatters in the mullion window, and an arm comes through and releases the catch. Enter an elderly **Burglar**. *He has great character, but is in need of extensive repair and modernisation.*

Burglar   No bars, no burglar alarm. They ought to be prosecuted for incitement . . .

He becomes aware of the others.

Selsdon   No?

Lloyd   No. Not yet. Thank you, Selsdon.

Selsdon   I thought I heard my name.

Lloyd   No, no, no. Back to sleep, Selsdon. Another ten pages before the big moment.

Selsdon   I'm so sorry.

Lloyd   Not at all. Nice to see you. Poppy, put the glass back in the window.

Enter **Poppy**. *She puts the glass back.*

Lloyd   And, Selsdon . . .

Selsdon   Yes?

Lloyd   Beautiful performance.

Selsdon   Oh, how kind of you. I don't think I'm quite there yet, though.

Exit **Selsdon** *through the window.*

Lloyd   He even remembered the line.

Frederick   All right, I see all that.

Lloyd (*faintly*)   Oh, no!

Frederick   I just don't know why I take them.

Lloyd *comes up on stage.*

Lloyd   Freddie, love, why does anyone do anything? Why does that other idiot walk out through the front door holding two plates of sardines? (*To* **Garry**.) I'm not getting at you, love.

Garry   Of course not, love. (*To* **Frederick**.) I mean, why do I? (*To* **Lloyd**.) I mean, right, when you come to think about it, why *do* I?

Lloyd   Who knows? The wellsprings of human action are deep and cloudy. (*To* **Frederick**.) Maybe something happened to you as a very small child which made you frightened to let go of groceries.

Belinda   Or it could be genetic.

Garry   Yes, or it could be, you know.

Lloyd   It could well be.

Frederick   Of course. Thank you. I understand all that. But . . .

Lloyd   Freddie, love, I'm telling you – I don't know. I don't think the author knows. I don't know why the author came into this industry in the first place. I don't know why any of us came into it.

Frederick   All the same, if you could just give me a reason I could keep in my mind . . .

Lloyd   All right, I'll give you a reason. You carry those groceries into the study, Freddie, honey, because it's just slightly after midnight, and we're not going to be finished before we open tomorrow night. Correction – before we open *tonight*.

Frederick *nods, rebuked, and exits into the study.* **Dotty** *silently follows him.* **Garry** *and* **Brooke** *go silently back into the bedroom.*

Lloyd *returns to the stalls.*

Lloyd   And on we go. From after Freddie's exit, *with* the groceries.

Belinda (*keeping her voice down*)   Lloyd, sweetheart, his wife left him this morning.

Lloyd   Oh. (*Pause.*) Freddie!

Enter **Frederick**, *still wounded, from the study.*

Lloyd   I think the point is that you've had a great fright when she mentions income tax, and you feel very insecure and exposed, and you want something familiar to hold on to.

Frederick (*with humble gratitude*)   Thank you, Lloyd. (*He clutches the groceries to his chest.*) That's most helpful.

Exit **Frederick** *into the study.*

Belinda (*to* **Lloyd**)   Bless you, my sweet.

Lloyd (*leaves the stage*)   And on we merrily go.

Exit **Belinda** *into the mezzanine bathroom.*

Lloyd   'Yes, but I could hear voices . . .'

Enter **Roger** *from the bedroom, still dressed, tying his tie.*

Roger   Yes, but I could hear voices!

Enter **Vicki** *from the bedroom in her underwear.*

Vicki   Voices? What sort of voices?

Roger   People's voices.

Vicki   But there's no one here.

Roger   Darling, I saw the door handle move! It could be someone from the office, checking up.

Vicki   I still don't see why you've got to put your tie on to look.

Roger   Mrs Crackett.

Vicki   Mrs Crackett?

Roger   One has to set an example to the staff.

Vicki (*looks over the bannisters*)   Oh, look, she's opened our sardines.

She moves to go downstairs. **Roger** *grabs her.*

Roger   Come back!

Vicki   What?

Roger   I'll fetch them! You can't go downstairs like that.

Vicki   Why not?

Roger   Mrs Crackett.

Vicki   Mrs Crackett?

Roger   One has certain obligations.

*Enter **Mrs Clackett** from the study. She is carrying the first plate of sardines.*

Mrs Clackett (*to herself*)   Sardines here. Sardines there. It's like a Sunday school outing.

Roger *pushes **Vicki** through the first available door, which happens to be the linen cupboard.*

Mrs Clackett   Oh, you're still poking around, are you?

Roger   Yes, still poking . . . well, still around.

Mrs Clackett   In the airing cupboard, were you?

Roger   No, no.

The linen cupboard door begins to open. He slams it shut.

Well, just checking the sheets and pillowcases. Going through the inventory.

He starts downstairs.

Mrs Blackett . . .

Mrs Clackett   Clackett, dear, Clackett.

She puts down the sardines beside the other sardines.

Roger   Mrs Clackett. Is there anyone else in the house, Mrs Clackett?

Mrs Clackett   I haven't seen no one, dear.

Roger   I thought I heard voices.

Mrs Clackett   Voices? There's no voices here, love.

Roger   I must have imagined it.

Philip (*off*)   Oh, good Lord above!

Roger, *with his back to her, picks up both plates of sardines.*

Roger   I beg your pardon?

Mrs Clackett   Oh, good Lord above, the study door's open.

She crosses and closes it. **Roger** *looks out of the window.*

Roger   There's another car outside! That's not Mr Hackham's, is it? Or Mr Dudley's?

Exit **Roger** *through the front door, holding both plates of sardines.*

Enter **Flavia** *from the mezzanine bathroom, carrying a hot water bottle. She sees the linen cupboard door swinging open as she passes, pushes it shut and turns the key.*

Flavia   Nothing but flapping doors in this house.

Exit **Flavia** *into the bedroom.*

Enter from the study **Philip**, *holding a tax demand and its envelope.*

Philip   '. . . final notice . . . steps will be taken . . . distraint . . . proceedings in court . . .'

Mrs Clackett   Oh yes, and that reminds me, a gentleman come about the house.

Philip   Don't tell me. I'm not here.

Mrs Clackett   He says he's got a lady quite aroused.

Philip   Leave everything to Squire, Squire, Hackham and Dudley.

Mrs Clackett   All right, love. I'll let them go all over, shall I?

Philip   Let them do anything. Just so long as you don't tell anyone we're here.

Mrs Clackett   So I'll just sit down and turn on the . . . sardines, I've forgotten the sardines! I don't know – if it wasn't fixed to my shoulders I'd forget what day it was.

Exit **Mrs Clackett** *to the service quarters.*

Philip   I didn't get this! I'm not here. I'm in Spain. But if I didn't get it I didn't open it.

Enter **Flavia** *from the bedroom. She is holding the dress that* **Vicki** *arrived in.*

Flavia   Darling, I never had a dress like this, did I?

Philip (*abstracted*)   Didn't you?

Flavia   I shouldn't buy anything as tarty as this . . . Oh, it's not something you gave me, is it?

Philip   I should never have touched it.

Flavia   No, it's lovely.

Philip   Stick it down. Put it back. Never saw it.

Exit **Philip** *into study.*

Flavia   Well, I'll put it in the attic, with all the other things you gave me that are too precious to wear.

Exit **Flavia** *along the upstairs corridor.*

Enter **Roger** *through the front door, still carrying both plates of sardines.*

Roger   All right, all right . . . Now the study door's open again! What's going on?

He puts the sardines down – one plate on the telephone table, where it was before, one near the front door – and goes towards the study, but stops at the sound of urgent knocking overhead.

Knocking!

Knocking.

Upstairs!

He runs upstairs. Knocking.

Oh my God, there's something in the airing cupboard!

He unlocks it and opens it. Enter **Vicki**.

Roger   Oh, it's you.

Vicki   Of course it's me! You put me in here! In the dark! With all black sheets and things!

Roger   But, darling, why did you lock the door?

Vicki   Why did *I* lock the door? Why did *you* lock the door!

Roger   *I* didn't lock the door!

Vicki   *Someone* locked the door!

Roger   Anyway, we can't stand here like this.

Vicki   Like what?

Roger   In your underwear.

Vicki   OK, I'll take it off.

Roger   In here, in here!

He ushers her into the bedroom.

Only she remains on, blinking anxiously and peering about the floor. **Garry** *waits for her, holding the bedroom door open.*

Enter **Philip** *from the study, holding the tax demand, the envelope, and a tube of glue.*

Philip   Darling, this glue. Is it the sort you can never get unstuck . . . ?

Lloyd   Hold it.

Philip   Oh, Mrs Clackett's made us some sardines.

Lloyd   Hold it. We have a problem.

Frederick (*to* **Brooke**)   Oh, bad luck! Which one is it this time?

Brooke   Left.

Garry (*calling to people, off*)   It's the left one, everybody!

Omnes (*off*)   Left one!

Enter **Dotty**, **Belinda**, *and* **Poppy**.

Frederick   It could be anywhere.

Garry (*looks over the edge of the gallery*)   It could have gone over the thing and fallen down, you know, and then bounced somewhere else again.

Brooke *comes downstairs. They all search hopelessly.*

Poppy   Where did you last see it?

Belinda   She *didn't* see it, poor sweet! It was in her eye!

Garry (*coming downstairs*)   It was probably on 'Why did I lock the door?' She opens her eyes very sort of, you know. Don't you, my sweet? I always feel I ought to rush forward and –

He rushes forward, hands held out.

Dotty   Mind where you put your feet, my love.

Frederick   Yes, everyone look under their feet.

Garry   No one move their feet.

Belinda   Everyone put their feet back exactly where they were.

Frederick   Pick your feet up one by one.

They all trample about, looking under their feet, except **Brooke**, *who crouches with her good eye at floor level.* **Lloyd** *comes up on stage.*

Lloyd   Brooke, love, is this going to happen during a performance? We don't want the audience to miss their last buses and trains.

Belinda   She'll just carry on. Won't you, my love?

Frederick   But can she see anything without them?

Lloyd   Can she hear anything without them?

Brooke (*suddenly realising that she is being addressed*)   Sorry?

Roger   Someone in the bathroom, filling hot-water bottles.

Exit **Roger** *into the mezzanine bathroom.*

Vicki (*anxious*)   You don't think there's something creepy going on?

Exit **Vicki** *into the mezzanine bathroom.*

Enter **Flavia** *along the upstairs corridor.*

Flavia   Darling, are you coming to bed or aren't you?

Exit **Flavia** *into the bedroom.*

Roger   What did you say?

Vicki   I didn't say anything.

Roger   I mean, first the door handle. Now the hot-water bottle . . .

Vicki   I can feel goose pimples all over.

Roger   Yes, quick, get something round you.

Vicki   Get the covers over our heads.

Roger *is about to open the bedroom door.*

Roger   Just a moment. What did I do with those sardines?

He goes downstairs. **Vicki** *makes to follow.*

Roger   You – wait here.

Vicki (*uneasily*)   You hear all sorts of funny things about these old houses.

Roger   Yes, but this one has been extensively modernised throughout. I can't see how anything creepy would survive fired central heating and . . .

Vicki   What? What is it?

Roger *stares at the telephone table in silence.*

She straightens up sharply. Her head comes into abrupt contact with **Poppy**'s *face.*

Poppy   Ugh!

Brooke   Oh. Sorry.

Brooke *jumps up to see what damage she has done to* **Poppy**, *and steps backward on to* **Garry**'s *hand.*

Garry   Ugh!

Brooke   Sorry.

Dotty *hurries to his aid.*

Dotty   Oh my poor darling! (*To* **Brooke**.) You stood on his hand!

Frederick   Oh dear. (*He hurriedly clasps a handkerchief to his nose.*)

Belinda   Oh, look at Freddie, the poor love!

Lloyd   What's the matter with *him*?

Belinda   He's just got a little nosebleed, my sweet.

Lloyd   A nosebleed? No one touched him!

Belinda   No, he's got a thing about violence. It always makes his nose bleed.

Frederick (*from behind his handkerchief*)   I'm so sorry.

Lloyd   Brooke, sweetheart. . .

Brooke   I thought you said something to me.

Lloyd   Yes. (*He picks up a vase and hands it to her.*) Just go and hit the box-office manager with this and you'll have finished off live theatre in Weston-super-Mare.

Brooke   Anyway, I've found it.

Belinda   She's found it!

Dotty   Where was it, love?

Brooke In my eye.

Garry In her eye!

Belinda (*hugging her*) Well done, my sweet.

Lloyd Not in your left eye?

Brooke It had gone round the side.

Belinda I knew it hadn't gone far. Are you all right, Poppy, my sweet?

Poppy I think so.

Belinda Freddie?

Frederick Fine, fine. (*He gets to his feet, looks in his handkerchief, and has to sit down again.*) I'm so sorry.

Lloyd *Now* what?

Belinda He's just feeling a little faint, my love. He's got this thing about . . . (*She tries to demonstrate.*)

Lloyd This thing about what?

Belinda Well, I won't say the word.

Frederick *gets to his feet.*

Lloyd You mean blood?

Frederick Oh dear. (*He has to sit down again.*)

Belinda (*to* **Frederick**) We all understand, my precious.

Lloyd All right, clear the stage. Walking wounded carry the stretcher cases.

Lloyd *returns to the stalls,* **Dotty** *to the service quarters,* **Poppy** *to the wings.* **Garry** *and* **Brooke** *go upstairs.* **Belinda** *helps* **Frederick** *to his feet.*

Lloyd Right, then. On we bloodily stagger.

Frederick *has to reach for a chair again.*

Lloyd Oh, sorry, Freddie. Let me rephrase that. On we blindly stumble. Brooke, I withdraw that.

Exit **Belinda** *along the upstairs corridor,* **Frederick** *into study.*

Lloyd From your exit, anyway. 'OK, I'll take it off . . . In here, in here.' Where's Selsdon?

Garry Selsdon!

Lloyd Selsdon!

Enter **Selsdon** *through the front door.*

Selsdon I think she might have dropped it out here somewhere.

Lloyd Good. Keep looking. Only another five pag Selsdon.

Exit **Selsdon** *through the front door.*

Lloyd 'Anyway, we can't stand here like this. – what?. – In your underwear. – OK, I'll take it off.

Roger In here, in here!

He ushers her into the bedroom.

Enter **Philip** *from the study, holding the tax demand, and a tube of glue.*

Philip Darling, this glue. Is it the sort you unstuck . . . ? Oh, Mrs Clackett's made us so

Exit **Philip** *into the study with the tax demand, e one of the plates of sardines from the telephone tabl*

Enter **Roger** *from the bedroom, holding the hot up and down the landing.*

Enter **Vicki** *from the bedroom.*

Vicki Now what?

Roger A hot-water bottle! *I* didn't p

Vicki *I* didn't put it there.

The bedroom door opens, and **Flavia** *puts* **Roger**'s *flight bag on the table outside without looking round. The door closes again.*

Vicki   What's happening?

Roger   The sardines. They've gone.

Vicki   Perhaps there is something funny going on. I'm going to get into bed and put my head under the . . .

She freezes at the sight of the flight bag.

Roger   I put them there. Or was it *there*?

Vicki   Bag . . .

Vicki *runs down the stairs to* **Roger**, *who is directly underneath the gallery.*

Roger   I suppose Mrs Sprockett must have taken them away again . . . What? What is it?

Vicki   Bag!

Roger   Bag?

Vicki   Bag! Bag!

Vicki *drags* **Roger** *silently back towards the stairs.*

Enter **Flavia** *from the bedroom with the box of files. She picks up the flight bag as well and takes them both off along the upstairs corridor.*

Roger   What do you mean, bag, bag?

Vicki   Bag! Bag! Bag!

Roger   What bag?

Vicki *sees the empty table outside the bedroom door.*

Vicki   No bag!

Roger   No bag?

Vicki   Your bag! Suddenly! Here! Now – gone!

Roger   It's in the bedroom. I put it in the bedroom.

Exit **Roger** *into the bedroom.*

Vicki   Don't go in there!

Enter **Roger** *from the bedroom.*

Roger   The box!

Vicki   The box!

Roger   They've both gone!

Vicki   Oh! My files!

Roger   What on earth's happening? Where's Mrs Spratchett?

He starts downstairs. **Vicki** *follows him.*

Roger   You wait in the bedroom.

Vicki   No! No! No!

She runs downstairs.

Roger   At least put your dress on!

Vicki   I'm not going in there!

Roger   I'll fetch it for you, I'll fetch it for you!

Exit **Roger** *into the bedroom.*

Vicki   Yes, quick – let's get out of here!

Enter **Roger** *from the bedroom.*

Roger   Your dress has gone.

Vicki   I'm never going to see Basingstoke again!

Roger *goes downstairs.*

Roger   Don't panic! Don't panic! There's some perfectly rational explanation for all this. I'll fetch Mrs Splotchett and she'll tell us what's happening. You wait here . . . You can't stand here looking like that . . . Wait in the study . . . Study, study, study!

Exit **Roger** *into the service quarters.*

Vicki *opens the study door. There's a roar of exasperation from* **Philip**, *off. She turns and flees.*

Vicki   Roger! There's a strange figure in there! Where are you?

There is another cry from **Philip**, *off.*

Exit **Vicki** *blindly through the front door.*

Enter **Philip** *from the study. He is holding the tax demand in his right hand and one of the plates of sardines in his left.*

Philip   Darling, I know this is going to sound silly, but . . .

He struggles to get the tax demand unstuck from his fingers, encumbered by the plate of sardines.

Enter **Flavia** *along the upstairs corridor, carrying various pieces of bric-a-brac.*

Flavia   Darling, if we're not going to bed I'm going to clear out the attic.

Philip   I can't come to bed! I'm glued to a tax demand!

Flavia   Darling, why don't you put the sardines down?

Philip *puts the plate of sardines down on the table. But when he takes his hand away the sardines come with it.*

Philip   Darling, I'm stuck to the sardines!

Flavia   Darling, don't play the fool. Get that bottle marked poison in the downstairs loo. That eats through anything.

Exit **Flavia** *along the upstairs corridor.*

Philip (*flapping the tax demand*)   I've heard of people getting *stuck* with a problem, but this is ridiculous.

Exit **Philip** *into the downstairs bathroom.*

Pause.

Lloyd   Selsdon . . . ? You're on, Selsdon. We're there. The moment's arrived . . .

Belinda (*off*)   It's all right, love. He's coming, he's coming . . .

Lloyd   But his arm should be coming through that window even before Freddie's off!

A pane of glass shatters in the mullion window and an arm comes through and releases the catch.

Lloyd   Ah. And here it is.

The window opens and through it appears an elderly **Burglar**. *He has great character, but is in need of extensive repair and modernisation.*

Burglar   No bars, no burglar alarm. They ought to be prosecuted for incitement.

He climbs in.

Lloyd   All right, Selsdon, hold it. Let's take it again.

Burglar   No, but sometimes it makes me want to sit down and weep. When I think I used to do banks! When I remember I used to do bullion vaults!

Lloyd   Hold it, Selsdon. Hold it!

Burglar   What am I doing now?

Lloyd   *Hold it!*

Enter **Poppy** *from the wings.*

Burglar   I'm breaking into paper bags!

Poppy   Lloyd wants you to hold it.

Enter **Belinda**.

Burglar   Right, what are they offering . . . ?

Belinda   Stop, Selsdon, my love! Wait, my precious!

Selsdon *stops, restrained at last by* **Belinda**'s *hand on his arm.*

Lloyd   It's like Myra Hess playing on through the air raids.

Selsdon   Stop?

Poppy   Stop.

Belinda   Stop.

Lloyd   Thank you, Belinda. Thank you, Poppy.

Exeunt **Belinda** *and* **Poppy**.

Lloyd   Selsdon . . .

Selsdon   I met Myra Hess once.

Lloyd   I think he can hear better than I can.

Selsdon   I beg your pardon?

Lloyd   From your entrance, please, Selsdon.

Selsdon   Well, it was during the war, at a charity show in Sunderland . . .

Lloyd   Thank you! Poppy!

Selsdon   Oh, not for me. It stops me sleeping.

Enter **Poppy** *from the wings*.

Lloyd   Put the glass back once more.

Selsdon   Come on again?

Lloyd   Right. Only, Selsdon . . .

Selsdon   Yes?

Lloyd   A little sooner, Selsdon. A shade earlier. A touch closer to yesterday. All right? Freddie!

Enter **Frederick**.

Lloyd (*to* **Selsdon**)   Start moving as soon as Freddie opens the door. (*To* **Frederick**.) What's the line?

Frederick   'I've heard of people getting *stuck* with a problem, but this is ridiculous.'

Lloyd   Start moving as soon as you hear the line, 'I've heard of people getting stuck with a *problem* . . .'

Frederick   'Stuck with a *problem*'?

Lloyd   'Stuck with a *problem*, but this is ridiculous.' And I want your arm through that window. Right?

Selsdon   Say no more. May I make a suggestion, though? Should I perhaps come on a little earlier?

Lloyd   Selsdon . . .

Selsdon   Only there does seem to be something of a hiatus between Freddie's exit and my entrance.

Lloyd   No, Selsdon. Listen. Don't worry. I've got it.

Selsdon   Yes?

Lloyd   How about coming on a little earlier?

Selsdon   We're obviously thinking along the same lines.

Exit **Selsdon** *through the window.*

Lloyd   Am I putting him on or is he putting me on? Right, Freddie, from your exit.

Philip (*flapping the tax demand*)   I've heard of people getting stuck with a *problem*, but this is ridiculous.

Exit **Philip** *into downstairs bathroom.*

Enter **Burglar** *as before, but on time.*

Burglar   No bars, no burglar alarms. They ought to be prosecuted for incitement.

He climbs in.

No, but sometimes it makes me want to sit down and weep. When I think I used to do banks! When I remember I used to do bullion vaults! What am I doing now? I'm breaking

---

into paper bags! So what are they offering? (*He peers at the television.*) One microwave oven.

He unplugs it and puts it on the sofa.

What? Fifty quid? Hardly worth lifting it.

He inspects the paintings and ornaments.

Junk . . . Junk . . . If you insist . . .

He pockets some small item.

Where's his desk? No, they all say the same thing . . . They all say the same thing . . .

Selsdon Yes? Line?

Poppy (*off*) 'It's hard to adjust to retirement.'

Selsdon What?

Lloyd (*wearily*) 'It's hard to adjust to retirement.'

Seldon Hard to what?

Others (*variously, off*) 'Adjust to retirement.'

Selsdon It's also very hard to hear if everyone talks at once.

Exit **Burglar** *into the study.*

Enter **Roger** *from the service quarters, followed by* **Mrs Clackett**, *who is holding another plate of sardines.*

Roger . . . And the prospective tenant naturally wishes to know if there is any previous history of paranormal phenomena.

Mrs Clackett Oh, yes, dear, it's all nice and paranormal.

Roger I mean, has anything ever dematerialised before? Has anything ever . . . ?

He sees the television set on the sofa.

. . . flown about?

Mrs Clackett *puts the sardines down on the telephone table, moves the television set back and closes the front door.*

Mrs Clackett   Flown about? No, the things move themselves on their own two feet, just like they do in any house.

Roger   I'd better warn the prospective tenant. She is inspecting the study.

He opens the study door and then closes it again.

There's a man in there!

Mrs Clackett   No, no, there's no one in the house, love.

Roger (*opening the study door*)   Look! Look! He's . . . *searching for* something.

Mrs Clackett (*glancing briefly*)   I can't see no one.

Roger   You can't see him? But this is extraordinary! And where is my prospective tenant? I left her in there! She's gone! My prospective tenant has disappeared!

He closes the study door and looks round the living-room. He sees the sardines on the telephone table.

Oh my God.

Mrs Clackett   Now what?

Roger   There!

Mrs Clackett   Where?

Roger   The sardines!

Mrs Clackett   Oh, the sardines.

Roger   You can see the sardines?

Mrs Clackett   I can see the sardines.

Roger *touches them cautiously, then picks up the plate.*

Mrs Clackett   I can see the way they're going, too.

Roger   I'm not letting these sardines out of my hand. But where is my prospective tenant?

He goes upstairs, holding the sardines.

Mrs Clackett   I'm going to be opening sardines all night, in and out of here like a cuckoo on a clock.

Exit **Mrs Clackett** *into the service quarters.*

Roger   Vicki! Vicki!

Exit **Roger** *into the mezzanine bathroom.*

Enter **Burglar** *from the study, carrying an armful of silver cups, etc.*

Burglar   No, I miss the violence. I miss having other human beings around to terrify . . .

He dumps the silverware on the sofa and exits into the study.

Enter **Roger** *from mezzanine bathroom.*

Roger   Where's she gone? Vicki?

Exit **Roger** *into the bedroom.*

Enter **Burglar** *from the study, carrying* **Philip**'s *box and bag. He empties the contents of the box out behind the sofa, and loads the silverware into the box.*

Burglar   It's nice to hear a bit of shouting and screaming around you. All this silence gets you down . . .

Enter **Roger** *from the linen cupboard, still holding the sardines.*

Roger (*calls*)   Vicki! Vicki!

Exit **Roger** *into the linen cupboard.*

Burglar   I'm going to end up talking to myself . . .

Exit the **Burglar** *into study, unaware of* **Roger**.

Enter **Philip** *from the downstairs bathroom. His right hand is still stuck to the tax demand, his left to the plate of sardines.*

Philip   Darling, this stuff that eats through anything. It eats through *trousers*!

He examines holes burnt in the front of them.

Darling, if it eats through trousers, you don't think it goes on and eats through . . . Listen, darling, I think I'd better get these trousers off! (*He begins to do so, as best he can.*) Darling, quick, this is an emergency! I mean, if it eats through absolutely anything . . . Darling, I think I can feel it! I think it's eating through . . . absolutely everything!

Enter **Roger** *from the bedroom, still holding the sardines.*

Roger   There's something evil in this house.

Philip *pulls up his trousers.*

Philip (*aside*)   The Inland Revenue!

Roger (*sees* **Philip**, *frightened*)   He's back!

Philip   No!

Roger   No?

Philip   I'm not here.

Roger   He's not there!

Philip   I'm abroad.

Roger   He's walking abroad.

Philip   I must go.

Roger   Stay!

Philip   I won't, thank you.

Roger   Speak!

Philip   Only in the presence of my lawyer.

Roger   Only in the presence of your . . . ? Hold on. You're not from the other world!

Philip   Yes, yes – Marbella!

Roger   You're some kind of intruder!

Philip   Well, nice to meet you.

He waves goodbye with his right hand, then sees the tax demand on it and hurriedly puts it away behind his back.

I mean, have a sardine.

He offers the sardines on his left hand. His trousers, unsupported, fall down.

Roger   No, you're not! You're some kind of sex maniac! You've done something to Vicki! I'm going to come straight downstairs . . . !

Roger *comes downstairs and dials 999.*

Philip   Oh, you've got some sardines. Well, if there's nothing I can offer you . . .

Roger   This is plainly a matter for the police! (*Into the phone.*) Police!

Philip   . . . I think I'll be running along.

He runs, his trousers still round his ankles, out through the front door.

Roger   Come back . . . ! (*Into the phone.*) Hello – police? Someone has broken into my house! Or rather someone has broken into someone's house . . . No, but he's a sex maniac! I left a young woman here and what's happened to her no one knows!

Enter **Vicki** *through the window.*

Vicki   There's a man lurking in the undergrowth!

Roger (*into the phone*)   Sorry . . . the young woman has reappeared. (*Hand over phone.*) Are you all right?

Vicki   No, he almost saw me!

Roger (*into the phone*)   He almost saw her . . . Yes, but he's a burglar as well! He's taken our things!

Vicki (*finds* **Philip**'s *bag and box*)   The things are here.

Roger (*into the phone*)   The things have come back. So we're just missing a plate of sardines.

Vicki (*finding the sardines left near the front door by* **Roger**) Here are the sardines.

Roger (*into the phone*)   And we've found the sardines.

Vicki   This is the police? You want the police here? In my underwear?

Roger (*into the phone*)   So what am I saying? I'm saying, let's say no more about it. (*He puts the phone down.*) I thought something terrible had happened to you!

Vicki   It has! I know him!

Roger   You know him?

Vicki   He's dealt with by our office!

Roger   He's just an ordinary sex maniac.

Vicki   Yes, but he mustn't see me like this! You have to keep up certain standards if you work for Inland Revenue!

Roger   Well, put something on!

Vicki   I haven't got anything!

Roger   There must be something in the bathroom!

He picks up the box and bag, and leads the way.

Bring the sardines!

She picks up the sardines. Exeunt **Roger** *and* **Vicki** *into the downstairs bathroom.*

Enter the **Burglar** *from the study and dumps more booty.*

Burglar   Right, that's downstairs tidied up a bit. (*He starts upstairs.*) Just give the upstairs a quick going-over for them.

Exit the **Burglar** *into the mezzanine bathroom.*

Enter **Vicki**, *holding the sardines and a white bathmat, and* **Roger**, *carrying the box and bag, from the downstairs bathroom.*

Vicki   A *bathmat?*

Roger   Better than nothing!

Vicki   I can't go around in front of our taxpayers wearing a *bathmat*!

Roger   The bedroom, then! There must be something in the bedroom!

He leads the way upstairs.

Vicki   No, no, no, no! I'm not going in that bedroom again!

Roger   *I'll* look in the bedroom. You look in the other bathroom.

Exit **Roger** *into the bedroom and* **Vicki** *into the mezzanine bathroom.*

Enter **Philip** *through the front door.*

Philip   Darling! Help! Where are you?

Enter **Vicki** *from the mezzanine bathroom.*

Vicki   Roger! Roger!

Exit **Philip** *hurriedly, unseen by* **Vicki**, *into the downstairs bathroom.*

Vicki   There's someone in the bathroom now!

Vicki *runs towards the bedrooms, then stops.*

Flavia (*off*)   Oh, darling, I'm finding such lovely things . . . !

Vicki *turns and runs downstairs instead, as* **Flavia** *enters along the upstairs corridor, absorbed in the china tea service she is carrying.*

Vicki *exits hurriedly into the downstairs bathroom.*

Flavia   Do you remember this china tea service –

Vicki *screams, off.*

Flavia   – that you gave me on the very first anniversary of our . . . ?

Enter **Vicki** *from the downstairs bathroom. She stops at the sight of* **Flavia***.*

Flavia   Who are you?

Vicki   Oh, *no* – it's his wife and dependents! (*She puts her hands over her face.*)

Enter **Philip** *from the downstairs bathroom, still with his hands encumbered, holding the bathmat now as well, and keeping his trousers up with his elbows.*

Philip   Excuse me, I think you've dropped your dress!

Flavia *gasps.* **Philip** *looks up at the gallery and sees her.*

Philip (*to* **Flavia**)   Where have you been? I've been going mad! Look at the state I'm in!

He holds up his hands to show **Flavia** *the state he is in and his trousers fall down. The tea service slips from* **Flavia***'s horrified hands, and rains down on the floor of the living-room below.* **Philip** *hurries towards the stairs, trousers round his ankles, his hands extended in supplication.*

Darling, honestly!

Vicki *flees before him, comes face to face with* **Flavia***, and takes refuge in the linen cupboard.*

Philip   She just burst into the room and her dress fell off!

Exit **Flavia***, with a cry of pain, along the upstairs corridor.*

Enter **Roger** *from the bedroom, directly in* **Philip***'s path.* **Philip** *holds up the bathmat in front of his face. He is invisible to* **Roger***, though, because the latter is holding up a white bedsheet.*

Roger   Here, put this sheet on for the moment while I see if there's something in the attic.

Roger *leaves* **Philip** *with the sheet and exits along upstairs corridor.*

Philip *turns to go back downstairs.*

Enter **Burglar** *from the mezzanine bathroom, holding two gold taps.*

Burglar   One pair gold taps . . . (*He stops at the sight of* **Philip**.) Oh, my Gawd!

Philip   Who are you?

Burglar   Me? Fixing the taps.

Philip   Tax? Income tax?

Burglar   That's right, governor. In come new taps . . . out go old taps.

Exit **Burglar** *into the mezzanine bathroom.*

Philip   Tax-inspectors everywhere!

Roger (*off*)   Here you are!

Philip   The other one!

Exit **Philip** *into the bedroom, holding the bathmat in front of his face.*

Enter **Roger** *along the upstairs corridor holding* **Vicki***'s dress.*

Roger   I've found your dress! It came flying out of the attic at me!

Exit **Roger** *into mezzanine bathroom.*

Enter **Philip** *from the bedroom, trying to pull the bathmat off his head.*

Philip   Darling! I've got her dress stuck to my head now!

Enter **Roger** *from the mezzanine bathroom.*

Exit **Philip** *into the bedroom.*

Roger   Another intruder!

Enter the **Burglar** *from the mezzanine bathroom.*

Burglar   Just doing the taps, governor.

Roger   Attacks? Not attacks on women?

Burglar   Try anything, governor, but I'll do the taps on the bath first.

Exit **Burglar** *into the mezzanine bathroom.*

Roger   Sex maniacs everywhere! Where is Vicki? Vicki . . . ?

Exit **Roger** *into the downstairs bathroom.*

Enter **Burglar** *from the mezzanine bathroom, heading for the front door.*

Burglar   People everywhere! I'm off. A tax on women? I don't know, they'll put a tax on anything these days.

Enter **Roger** *from the downstairs bathroom. The* **Burglar** *stops.*

Roger   If I can't find her, you're going to be in trouble, you see.

Burglar   WC? I'll fix it.

Exit **Burglar** *into the mezzanine bathroom again.*

Roger   Vicki . . . ?

Exit **Roger** *through the front door.*

Enter **Philip** *from the bedroom. The bathmat is still on his head, but is now arranged like a burnous, and he is wrapped in a white bedsheet.*

Enter **Vicki** *from the linen cupboard, enrobed from head to foot in a black bedsheet. They both quietly close the doors behind them.*

Vicki⎱   Roger!
Philip⎰   Darling!

They see each other and start back.

Enter **Roger** *through the front door.*

Roger   Sheikh! I thought you were coming at four? And this is your charming wife? So you want to see over the house now, do you, Sheikh? Right. Well. Since you're upstairs already . . .

Roger *goes upstairs.*

Enter **Flavia** *along the upstairs corridor, carrying a vase.*

Flavia   Him and his floozie! I'll break this over their heads!

Roger   . . . let's start downstairs.

Roger, **Philip** *and* **Vicki** *go downstairs.*

Flavia   Who are you? Who are these creatures?

Roger (*to* **Philip** *and* **Vicki**)   I'm sorry about this. I don't know who she is. No connection with the house, I assure you.

Enter **Mrs Clackett** *from the service quarters, with another plate of sardines.* **Roger** *advances to introduce her.*

Roger   Whereas this good lady with the sardines, on the other hand . . .

Mrs Clackett   No other hands, thank you, not in my sardines, 'cause this time I'm eating them.

Roger   . . . is fully occupied with her sardines, so perhaps the toilet facilities would be of more interest.

He ushers **Philip** *and* **Vicki** *away from* **Mrs Clackett** *towards the mezzanine bathroom.*

Flavia   Mrs Clackett, who are these people?

Mrs Clackett   Oh, we get them all the time, love. They're just Arab sheets.

Roger   I'm sorry about this. (*He opens the door to the mezzanine bathroom.*) But in here . . .

Flavia   *Arab* sheets?

Exit **Flavia** *into the bedroom.*

Roger   In here we have . . .

Enter the **Burglar** *from the mezzanine bathroom.*

Burglar   Ballcocks, governor. Your ballcocks have gone.

Roger   We have him.

Enter **Flavia** *from the bedroom.*

Flavia   They're *Irish* sheets! Irish linen sheets off my own bed!

Mrs Clackett   Oh, the thieving devils!

Roger   In the *study*, however . . .

Mrs Clackett   You give me that sheet, you devil!

She seizes the nearest sheet, and it comes away in her hand to reveal **Vicki**.

Oh, and there she stands in her smalls, for all the world to see!

Roger   It's you!

Flavia   It's her!

Flavia *comes downstairs menacingly.*

Exit **Philip** *discreetly into the study.*

Burglar   It's my little girl!

Vicki   Dad!

Flavia *stops.*

Enter **Philip** *from the study in amazement.* (*He is now played by a double –* **Tim**.)

Burglar   Our little Vicki, that ran away from home, I thought I'd never see again!

Mrs Clackett   Well, would you believe it?

Vicki (*to* **Burglar**)   What are you doing here like this?

Burglar   What are *you* doing here like *that*?

Vicki   Me? I'm taking our files on tax evasion to Inland Revenue in Basingstoke.

Philip/Tim   Agh!

He collapses behind the sofa, clutching at his heart, unnoticed by the others.

Flavia (*threateningly*)   So where's my other sheet?

Enter through the front door the most sought-after of all properties on the market today – a **Sheikh**. *He is wearing Arab robes and bears a strong resemblance to* **Philip**, *since he is also played by* **Frederick**.

Sheikh   Ah! A house of heavenly peace! I rent it!

Roger   Hold on, hold on . . . I know that face! (*Pulls the Sheik's burnous aside to reveal his face.*) He isn't a sheikh! He's that sex-maniac!

Flavia   Yes – it's my husband!

Sheikh   What?

They all fall upon him.

Frederick's *trousers are revealed to be around his ankles.*

Lloyd   Trousers!

Mrs Clackett   You take all the clean sheets! (*She tries to pull the robes off him.*)

Sheikh   What? What?

Lloyd   Trousers! Trousers!

Vicki   You snatch my bathmat! (*She tries to pull his burnous off him.*)

Sheikh   What? What? What?

Flavia   You toss me aside like a broken china doll! (*She hits him.*)

Lloyd   And to cap it all you've got your trousers on!

Everyone except **Selsdon** *finally comes to a halt.*

> **Burglar**   And what you're up to with my little girl down
> there in Basingstoke . . .

Even **Selsdon** *becomes aware that the action has ceased.*

Selsdon   Stop?

Belinda   Stop, stop.

Lloyd *comes up on stage.*

Lloyd   It's a question of authenticity, you see, Freddie. *Do*
Arab potentates wear trousers under their robes? I don't
know. Maybe they do. But not round their ankles, Freddie!
Not round their ankles!

Frederick   Sorry. It's just frightfully difficult doing a
quick change without a dresser.

Lloyd   Get Tim to help you. Tim! Where's Tim? Come
on, Tim! Tim!

Tim, *wearing the sheet as* **Philip**'s *double, gets to his feet and gazes
blearily at* **Lloyd**.

Tim   Sorry?

Lloyd   Oh, yes. You're acting.

Tim   I must have dropped off down there.

Lloyd   Never mind, Tim.

Tim   Do something?

Lloyd   No, let it pass. We'll just struggle through on our
own. Tim has a sleep behind the sofa, while all the rest of us
run round with our trousers round our ankles. OK,
Freddie? You'll just have to do the best you can. On we go,
then . . .

Frederick *hesitates.*

Lloyd   Some other problem, Freddie?

Frederick   Well, since we're stopped anyway.

Lloyd   Why did I ask?

Frederick   I mean, you know how stupid I am about plot.

Lloyd   I know, Freddie.

Frederick   May I ask another silly question?

Lloyd   All my studies in world drama lie at your disposal.

Frederick   I still don't understand why the Sheikh just happens to be Philip's double.

Garry   Because he comes in and we all think he's, you know, and we all, I mean, that's the joke.

Frederick   I see that.

Belinda   My sweet, the rest of the plot depends on it!

Frederick   I see that. But it *is* rather a coincidence, isn't it?

Lloyd   It *is* rather a coincidence, Freddie, yes. Until you reflect that there was an earlier draft of the play, now unfortunately lost to us. And in this the author makes it clear that Philip's father as a young man had travelled extensively in the Middle East.

Frederick   I see . . . I *see*!

Lloyd   You see?

Frederick   That's very interesting.

Lloyd   I thought you'd like that.

Frederick   But will the audience get it?

Lloyd   You must tell them, Freddie. Looks. Gestures. That's what acting's all about. OK?

Frederick   Yes. Thank you, Lloyd. Thank you.

Lloyd   And it will be even more powerful when you do it with no trousers.

Frederick   Of course. (*Takes his trousers off.*)

Lloyd   Right, can we just finish the act? From Belinda's beautiful line, 'You toss me aside like a broken china doll!'

Lloyd *returns to the stalls.*

I'm being so clever out here! What's going to be left of this show when I've gone off to do *Richard III* and you're up there on your own? Right – 'You toss me aside like a broken china doll!'

Flavia   You toss me aside like a broken china doll! (*She hits him.*)

Sheikh   What? What? What?

Burglar   And what you're up to with my little girl down there in Basingstoke I won't ask. But I'll tell you one thing, Vicki.

Pause.

Lloyd   Brooke!

Brooke   Sorry . . .

Lloyd   Your line. Come on, love, we're two lines away from the end of the act.

Brooke   I don't understand.

Lloyd   Give her the line!

Poppy (*off*)   'What's that, Dad?'

Brooke   Yes, but I don't understand.

Belinda   It's 'What's that, Dad?'

Selsdon   Yes, I say to you, 'I'll tell you one thing, Vicki' and you say to me, 'What's that, Dad?'

Brooke   I don't understand why the Sheikh looks like Philip.

Silence. Everyone waits for the storm. **Lloyd** *comes slowly up on stage.*

Lloyd   Poppy! Bring the book!

Enter **Poppy** *from the wings, with the book.*

Lloyd (*patiently*)   Is that the line, Poppy? 'I don't understand why the Sheikh looks like Philip'? Can we consult the author's text and make absolutely sure?

Poppy   Well, I think it's . . .

Lloyd (*with exquisite politeness*)   'What's that, Dad?' Right. That's the line, Brooke, love. We all know you've worked in very classy places up in London where they let you make the play up as you go along, but we don't want that kind of thing here, do we. Not when the author has provided us with such a considered and polished line of his own. Not at one o'clock in the morning. Not two lines away from the end of Act One. Not when we're just about to get a tea break before we all drop dead of exhaustion. We merely want to hear the line. (*Suddenly puts his mouth next to* **Brooke***'s ear and shouts.*) 'What's that, Dad?' (*All patience and politeness again.*) That's all. Nothing else. I'm not being unreasonable, am I?

Brooke *abruptly turns, runs upstairs and exits into the mezzanine bathroom.*

Lloyd   Exit? Does it say 'exit'?

The sound of **Brooke** *weeping, off, and running downstairs.*

Lloyd   Oh dear, now she's going to wash her lenses away.

Exit **Lloyd** *through the front door.*

Frederick (*chastened*)   Oh, good Lord.

Selsdon (*likewise*)   A little heavy with the sauce, I thought.

Garry   I thought it was going to be Poppy when he finally, you know.

Dotty   It's usually Poppy. Isn't it, love?

Poppy *smiles wanly.*

Frederick   I suppose that was all my fault.

Garry   But why pick on, you know?

Dotty   Yes, why Brooke?

Belinda   I thought it was quite sweet, actually.

Garry   Sweet?

Belinda   Trying to pretend they're not having a little thing together.

Dotty   A little thing? Lloyd and Brooke . . . ?

Belinda   Didn't you know?

Selsdon   Brooke and Lloyd?

Belinda   Where do you think they've been all weekend?

Frederick   Good Lord. You mean, that's why he wasn't here when poor old Tim . . .

He stops, conscious that **Tim** *is behind the sofa.*

Dotty   . . . put the set up back-to-front.

Belinda   Sh! Here they come!

Enter **Lloyd** *with his arm round* **Brooke**.

Lloyd   OK. All forgotten. I was irresistible.

Poppy   I think I'm going to be sick.

Exit **Poppy** *into the wings.*

Dotty   Oh, no!

Lloyd   Oh, for heaven's *sake*!

Exit **Lloyd** *after* **Poppy**.

Garry   You mean . . . ?

Selsdon   Her, too?

Frederick   Oh, great Scott!

Belinda   Well, that's something I *didn't* know.

Brooke   I think I'm going to faint.

Dotty   Yes, sit down, love!

They sit **Brooke** *down.*

Belinda   Quick – do your meditation.

Selsdon   Well, that's something *she* didn't know!

Belinda   Hush, love.

Dotty   Two weeks' rehearsal, that's all we've had.

Frederick   Whatever next?

Selsdon   *Most* exciting!

Belinda (*indicating* **Brooke**)   Sh!

Selsdon   Oh, yes. Sh!

Dotty   Here he comes.

Enter **Lloyd** *from the wings, subdued.*

Dotty   Is she all right, love?

Lloyd   She'll be all right in a minute. Something she ate, probably.

Garry (*indicating* **Brooke**)   Yes, this one's feeling a bit, you know.

Lloyd   I'm feeling a bit, you know, myself. I think I'm going to –

Belinda   Which?

Garry (*offering a chair*)   Faint?

Belinda (*offering a vase*)   Or be sick?

Lloyd (*subsides on to the chair*)   – need that tea break.

Dotty   You're certainly overdoing it at the moment, love.

Lloyd   So could we just have the last line of the act?

Selsdon   Me? Last line? Right.

Burglar   But I'll tell you one thing, Vicki.

Vicki (*with a murderous look at* **Lloyd**)   What's that, *Dad?*

Burglar   When all around is strife and uncertainty, there's nothing like a . . .

Selsdon   . . . what?

Poppy (*off, tearful*)   Oh . . . 'A good old-fashioned plate of sardines.'

Selsdon   What did she say?

Belinda   'A good old-fashioned plate . . .'

She hands him **Mrs Clackett***'s plate.*

Burglar   A good old-fashioned plate of . . .

Selsdon   . . . *what?*

Poppy *runs on with the book,* **Lloyd** *jumps to his feet,* **Tim** *jumps up from behind the sofa.*

Everyone *except* **Selsdon**   *Sardines!*

Tableau, with raised sardines. The tableau continues.

Lloyd   And *curtain!*

Poppy (*realises, sobs*)   Oh!

She runs hurriedly into the wings.

CURTAIN

Act Two

The living-room of the Brents' country home. Wednesday afternoon.

(Theatre Royal, Ashton-under-Lyne. Wednesday matinée,
13 February.)

But this time we are watching the action from behind; the whole set has
been turned through 180 degrees. All the doors can be seen — there is no
masking behind them. Two stairways lead up to the platform that gives
access to the doors on the upper level. Some of the scene inside the
living-room is visible through the full-length window. There are also
two doors in the backstage fabric of the theatre: one giving access to the
dressing-rooms, and the pass door into the auditorium. The usual
backstage furnishings, including the prompt corner and props table,
chairs for the actors, a fire-point with fire-buckets and fire-axe, etc.

Tim *is walking anxiously up and down in his dinner jacket.*

Poppy *is speaking into the microphone in the prompt corner.*

Poppy (*over the tannoy*)   Act One beginners, please. Your
calls, Miss Otley, Miss Ashton, Mr Lejeune, Mr Fellowes,
Miss Blair. Act One beginners, please.

Tim   And maybe Act One beginners is what we'll get.
What do you think?

Poppy (*to* **Tim**)   Oh, Dotty'll pull herself together now
we've called beginners. Now she knows she's got to be on
stage in five minutes. Won't she?

Tim   Will she?

Poppy   You know what Dotty's like.

Tim   We've only been on the road for a month! We've
only got to Ashton-under-Lyne! What's it going to be like by
the time we've got to Stockton-on-Tees?

Poppy   If only she'd speak!

Tim   If only she'd unlock her dressing-room door! Look, if Dotty won't go on . . .

Poppy   Won't go on?

Tim   If she won't.

Poppy   She will.

Tim   Of course she will.

Poppy   Won't she?

Tim   I'm sure she will. But if she *doesn't* . . .

Poppy   She must!

Tim   She will, she will. But if she *didn't* . . .

Poppy   I'd have five minutes to change. Four minutes.

Tim   If only she'd say something.

The pass door opens cautiously, and **Lloyd** *puts his head round. He closes it again at the sight of* **Poppy**.

Poppy   I'll have another go. Takes your mind off your own problems, anyway.

Exit **Poppy** *in the direction of the dressing-rooms.*

Lloyd *puts his head back round the door.*

Lloyd   Has she gone?

Tim   Lloyd! I didn't know you were coming today!

Lloyd *comes in. He is carrying a bottle of whisky.*

Lloyd   I wasn't. I haven't.

Tim   Anyway, thank God you're here!

Lloyd   I'm not. I'm in Aberystwyth. I'm in the middle of rehearsing *Richard III*.

Tim   Dotty and Garry . . .

Lloyd   I don't want anyone to know I'm in.

Tim No, but Dotty and Garry . . .

Lloyd I just want two hours alone and undisturbed with Brooke in her dressing-room between shows, then I'm on the 7.25 back to Wales. (*Gives* **Tim** *the whisky.*) This is for Brooke. Put it somewhere safe. Make sure Selsdon doesn't get his hands on it.

Tim Right. They've had some kind of row. . .

Lloyd Good, good. (*Takes money out of his wallet and gives it to* **Tim**.) There's a little flower shop across the road from the stage door. I want you to buy me some very large and expensive-looking flowers.

Tim Right. Now Dotty's locked herself in her dressing-room . . .

Lloyd Don't let Poppy see them. They're not for Poppy.

Tim No. And she won't speak to anyone . . .

Lloyd First house finishes just after five, yes? Second house starts at seven thirty?

Tim Lloyd, that's what I'm trying to tell you – there may not *be* a show!

Lloyd She hasn't walked out already?

Tim No one knows *what* she's doing! She's locked in her dressing-room! She won't speak to anyone!

Lloyd You've called beginners?

Tim Yes!

Lloyd I can't play a complete love scene from cold in five minutes. It's not dramatically possible.

Tim She's had bust-ups with Garry before, of course.

Lloyd Brooke's had a bust-up with Garry?

Tim Brooke? Not Brooke – Dotty!

Lloyd Oh, Dotty.

Tim   I mean, they had the famous bust-up the week before last, when we were playing Worksop.

Lloyd   Right, right, you told me on the phone.

Tim   She went out with this journalist bloke . . .

Lloyd   Journalist – yes, yes . . .

Tim   But you know Garry threatened to kill him?

Lloyd   Killed him, yes, I know. Listen, don't worry about Dotty – she's got money in the show.

Tim   Yes, but now it's happened again! Two o'clock this morning I'm woken up by this great banging on my door. It's Garry. Do I know where Dotty is? She hasn't come home.

Lloyd   Tim, let me tell you something about *my* life. I have the Duke of Buckingham on the phone to me for an hour after rehearsal every evening complaining that the Duke of Gloucester is sucking boiled sweets through his speeches. The Duke of Clarence is off for the entire week doing a commercial for Madeira. Richard himself – would you believe? – Richard III? (*He demonstrates.*) – has now gone down with a back problem. I keep getting messages from Brooke about how unhappy she is here and now she's got herself a doctor's certificate for nervous exhaustion – she's going to walk! I have no time to find or rehearse another Vicki. I have just one afternoon, while Richard is fitted for a surgical corset, to cure Brooke of nervous exhaustion, with no medical aids except a little whisky – you've got the whisky? – a few flowers – you've got the money for the flowers? – and a certain faded charm. So I haven't come to the theatre to hear about other people's problems. I've come to be taken out of myself and preferably not put back again.

Tim   Yes, but Lloyd . . .

Lloyd   Have you done the front-of-house calls?

Tim   Oh, the front-of-house calls!

Tim *hurries to the microphone in the prompt corner, still holding the money and whisky.*

Lloyd   And don't let Poppy see those flowers!

Exit **Lloyd** *through the pass door.*

Tim (*into microphone*)   Ladies and gentlemen, will you please take your seats. The curtain will rise in three minutes.

Enter **Poppy** *from the dressing-rooms.*

Poppy   We're going to be so late up!

Tim   No luck?

Poppy   Belinda's having a go. I haven't even started the front-of-house calls yet . . . Money? What's this for?

Tim   Nothing, nothing! (*He puts the money behind his back and automatically produces the whisky with the other hand.*)

Poppy   Whisky!

Tim   Oh . . . is it?

Poppy   Where did you find that?

Tim   Well . . .

Poppy   Up here? You mean Selsdon's hiding them round the stage now? (*She takes the whisky.*)

Tim   Oh . . .

Poppy   I'll put it in the ladies' loo. At least he won't go in there.

Enter **Belinda** *from the dressing-rooms.*

Poppy   No?

Belinda   You know what Dotty's like when she's like this. Freddie's trying now . . . (*She sees the whisky.*) Oh, no!

Poppy   He's hiding them round the stage now.

Enter **Frederick** *from the dressing-rooms.*

Poppy No?

Frederick No.

Belinda You didn't try for very long, my precious!

Frederick No, well . . . (*He sees the whisky.*) Oh dear.

Belinda He's hiding them on stage now.

Exit **Poppy** *to the dressing-rooms, holding the whisky.*

Frederick No, Garry came rushing out of his dressing-room in a great state. I couldn't quite understand what he was saying. I often feel with Garry that I must have missed something somewhere. You know how stupid I am about that kind of thing. But I think he was saying he wanted to kill me.

Belinda Oh, my poor sweet!

Frederick I thought I'd better leave him to it. I don't want to make things worse. He's all right, is he?

Belinda Who, Garry? Anything but, by the sound of it!

Frederick I mean, he's going on?

Tim Garry? *Garry's* going on. Of course he's going on. What's all this about *Garry* not going on?

Belinda Yes, because if you have to go on for Garry, Poppy can't go on for Dotty, because if Poppy goes on for Dotty, you'll have to be on the book!

Tim This is getting farcical.

Belinda Money.

Tim Money?

Belinda You're waving money around.

Tim Oh, that's for . . . Oh . . . !

Tim *hurriedly grabs his raincoat from a peg and exits into the dressing-rooms.*

Frederick   She's a funny woman, you know – Dotty. So up and down. She was perfectly all right last night.

Belinda   Last night?

Frederick   Yes, she took me for a drink after the show in some club she knows about.

Belinda   She was with *you*? You were with *her*?

Frederick   She was being very sympathetic about all my troubles.

Belinda   She's not going to sink her teeth into you! I won't let her!

Frederick   No, no, she couldn't have been nicer. In fact, she came back to my digs afterwards for a cup of tea and she told me all *her* troubles. Sat there until three o'clock this morning. I don't know *what* the landlady thought!

Enter **Poppy**.

Poppy   And another thing.

Belinda   Nothing else, my sweet!

Poppy   Where's Selsdon?

Belinda   It turns out that it's Freddie here who's the cause of all the . . . Selsdon?

Poppy   He's not in his dressing-room.

Belinda   Oh – I might have guessed!

Poppy   Oh – the front-of-house calls!

Belinda   You do the calls. I'll took for Selsdon.

Frederick   What shall I do?

Belinda (*firmly*)   Absolutely nothing at all.

Frederick   Right.

Belinda   You've done quite enough already, my pet.

Exit **Belinda** *to the dressing-rooms.*

Poppy (*into the microphone*)   Ladies and gentlemen, will you please take your seats. The curtain will rise in three minutes.

Enter **Tim** *from the dressing-rooms in his raincoat, carrying a large bunch of flowers.*

Tim   He wants to kill someone. (*He takes off his raincoat.*)

Poppy   *Selsdon* wants to kill someone?

Tim   Garry, Garry. . . Selsdon?

Poppy   We've lost him.

Tim   Oh, not again!

Poppy   Flowers!

Tim (*embarrassed*)   Oh . . . Well . . . They're just . . . You know . . .

Poppy (*taking them*)   Oh, Tim that's really sweet of you!

Tim   Oh . . . Well . . .

Poppy (*to* **Frederick**)   Isn't that sweet of him?

Frederick   Very charming.

She kisses **Tim**.

Poppy   I'll just look in the pub. (*She gives the flowers to* **Frederick**.) Hold these.

Exit **Poppy** *to the dressing-rooms.*

Tim   I'll take those. (*He takes the flowers.*) Oh, the front-of-house calls! Hold these. (*He gives the flowers back to* **Frederick**.)

Frederick   Oh, I think Poppy's done them.

Tim   She gave them two minutes, did she? I'll give them one minute. (*Into the microphone.*) Ladies and gentlemen, will you please take your seats. The curtain will rise in one minute.

He takes the flowers from **Frederick**.

Frederick   Oh dear, I think she said three minutes.

Tim   *Three* minutes? *I* said three minutes! *She* said three minutes?

Frederick   I think so.

Tim   Hold these. (*He gives* **Frederick** *the flowers. Into the microphone.*) Ladies and gentlemen, will you please take your seats. The curtain will rise in two minutes.

Enter **Belinda** *from the dressing-rooms, holding the bottle of whisky.*

Frederick   Any luck?

Belinda   No, but I found yet another bottle.

Frederick   Oh dear.

Tim   Oh . . .

Belinda   Hidden in the ladies' lavatory, would you believe.

Frederick   Oh, my Lord!

Tim (*takes it*)   Oxfam! I'll give it to Oxfam!

Poppy *runs in from the dressing-rooms.*

Poppy   He's not in the pub . . .

Belinda (*indicates the whisky to* **Poppy**)   No, he's hanging round ladies' lavatories.

Tim   I'd better get the spare gear on.

Exit **Tim** *to the dressing-rooms with the whisky.*

Poppy (*into the microphone*)   Ladies and gentlemen, will you please take your seats. The curtain will rise in two minutes.

Frederick   Oh dear – Tim's already told them two minutes.

Poppy   He's done two minutes? (*Into the microphone.*) Ladies and gentlemen, will you please take your seats. The curtain will rise in one minute.

*Enter **Lloyd** through the pass door.*

Lloyd   What the fuck is going on?

Belinda   Lloyd!

Frederick   Great Scott!

Poppy   I didn't know you were here!

Lloyd   I'm not here! I'm at the Aberystwyth Festival! But I can't sit out there and listen to 'two minutes . . . three minutes . . . one minute . . . two minutes'!

Belinda   My sweet, we're having great dramas downstairs!

Lloyd   We're having great dramas out there! (*To **Poppy**.*) This is the matinée, honey! There's old-age pensioners out there! 'The curtain will rise in three minutes' – we all start for the Gents. 'The curtain will rise in one minute' – we all come running out again. We don't know which way we're going!

Poppy   Lloyd, I've got to have a talk to you.

Lloyd (*kissing her*)   Of course, honey, of course. Looking forward to it.

Poppy   You got my message?

Lloyd   Many, many messages.

Poppy   Why didn't you answer?

Lloyd   I did! I have! I'm here!

Poppy   Lloyd, there's something I've got to tell you.

Lloyd   Go on, then.

Poppy   Well . . . (*She hesitates, embarrassed because other people can hear, then tries to keep her voice down.*) I went to the doctor today. . .

Enter **Brooke** *from the dressing-rooms, with the whisky.*

Belinda   Brooke!

Lloyd *hastily abandons* **Poppy**.

Lloyd (*to* **Poppy**)   Later, later. All right?

Brooke *holds up the whisky.*

Belinda   Oh, no! Not another one!

Brooke   In my dressing-room!

Belinda (*she takes the whisky*)   In your *dressing-room*? (*To* **Lloyd**.) It's getting completely out of control!

Frederick (*taking the whisky*)   I'll give it to Oxfam, with the other one.

Lloyd (*holds out his hand for the whisky*)   I'll do it. Thank you.

Brooke (*sees him*)   Lloyd! (*Peers.*) Lloyd?

Lloyd   Got it in one. (*Kisses her.*)

Brooke   You got my message?

Lloyd   And came running, honey, and came running.

Brooke   Lloyd, we've got to have a talk.

Lloyd   We're *going* to have a talk, my love.

Brooke   When?

Lloyd   Later, yes? Later.

He goes to take the whisky from **Frederick**, *but is distracted by seeing the flowers that* **Frederick** *is holding.*

Flowers?

Frederick   Oh, yes, sorry. (*He gives the flowers to* **Poppy**.)

Poppy   Tim bought them for me. (*She puts them on her desk in the prompt corner.*)

Lloyd   *Tim?* Bought them for *you?*

Poppy   To cheer me up. (*Anxiously.*) Lloyd . . .

Lloyd   Nothing more, just for the moment. Thank you. (*To* **Frederick**.) Strangle Tim for me when you see him, will you?

Frederick   Right.

Lloyd *goes towards the pass door.*

Belinda   But what about Dotty?

Lloyd   I don't want to hear about Dotty.

Frederick   And Garry?

Lloyd   Not about Garry, either.

Belinda   What about Selsdon?

Lloyd   Listen, I think this show is beyond the help of a director. You just do it. I'll sit out there in the dark with a bag of toffees and enjoy it. OK? 'One minute' was the last call, if your memory goes back that far.

Brooke   Lloyd!

Poppy   Wait!

Lloyd *exits through the pass door.* **Poppy** *and* **Brooke** *jostle to follow him.*

Brooke (*to* **Poppy**)   Excuse *me!*

Poppy   I've got to talk to him!

Frederick (*separating them*)   Girls, girls!

Brooke (*indicates the dressing-rooms*)   I've a good mind to put my coat on and walk out of that door right here and now.

Frederick   Listen, if you don't feel up to performing I'm sure Poppy would always be happy to have a bash on your behalf.

Brooke   I *beg* your pardon?

Poppy   Honestly!

Belinda (*firmly*)   Brooke, you sit down and do your meditation. Poppy, you go and see what's happening with Dotty and Garry.

Brooke *reluctantly sits down on the floor. Exit* **Poppy** *to the dressing-rooms.*

Belinda   Freddie, my sweet precious . . .

Frederick   Did I say something wrong?

Enter **Selsdon** *hurriedly through the pass door.*

Selsdon   Where's Tim?

Belinda   Selsdon! My sweet! Where have you been?

Frederick   Are you all right? (*He puts out a sympathetic hand, then realises that it contains the whisky bottle.*) Oh dear. (*He hurriedly puts it out of sight behind his back.*)

Belinda   We've been looking for you everywhere!

Selsdon   Oh, yes, everywhere. In front – manager's office – bar. Not a sign of him.

Belinda   He's looking for you in the dressing-rooms.

Selsdon   That's right! Great shindig been going on down there. I thought Tim ought to know about it.

Belinda   My love, I think he's heard.

Selsdon   Oh, everything! Oh, he really went for her! 'I know when you've got your eye on someone!'

Frederick   Oh dear, Dotty's got her eye on someone, has she?

Selsdon   'I've seen you creeping off into corners with that poor halfwit.'

Frederick   Which poor halfwit?

Belinda   Never mind, my love.

Frederick   Not *Tim*?

Belinda   No, no, no.

Frederick   But who else is there? Apart from me?

Enter **Poppy** *from the dressing-rooms.*

Poppy   I think they're coming.

Belinda   They're coming!

Frederick   They're coming!

Selsdon   I knew they wouldn't.

Poppy   And you're *here*!

Selsdon   Oh, yes, every word!

Poppy   Right. (*Into the microphone.*) Ladies and gentlemen, will you please take your seats. The performance is about to begin.

Enter **Tim** *from the dressing-rooms, in* **Burglar***'s costume.*

Tim   They're coming.

Belinda   And we've found Selsdon.

Tim (*to* **Selsdon**)   How did *you* get here?

Selsdon   How? Through the wall!

Tim (*into the microphone*)   Ladies and gentlemen, will you please take your seats.

Poppy   I've done it!

Tim (*into the microphone*)   The performance is about to . . .

Poppy   I've done it, I've done it!

Tim (*to* **Poppy**)   Done it? Done 'about to begin'?

Poppy   Yes! About to begin, about to begin!

Tim (*into the microphone*)   is about to . . . is about to begin *at any moment.*

Belinda   Poor Lloyd! He'll choke on his toffees.

Selsdon   No, the walls are very thin, you see. 'I'm absolutely sick to death of it,' she cries . . . (*Takes in what* **Tim** *is wearing.*) Am I setting a bit of a trend?

Tim (*realises*)   Oh. . .

Belinda (*quickly, snatching* **Tim**'s **Burglar** *cap off*) Understudy rehearsal, my love.

Selsdon   Oh, for Garry, yes – very timely. 'You try to give some poor devil a leg up,' she says.

Enter **Garry** *from the dressing-rooms.*

Belinda   Garry, my sweet!

Selsdon   Or she may have said, 'a leg over. . .' Oh, and here he is.

Frederick (*to* **Garry**)   Are you all right?

Frederick *collects the box and the flight bag from the props table and smilingly offers them to* **Garry***, who snatches them angrily.*

Selsdon   What does he say?

Belinda   He's not saying anything, Selsdon, my sweet.

Selsdon   Very sensible. Only stir it up again. 'I've seen you giving him little nods and smiles!' – that's what he kept saying.

Enter **Dotty** *from the dressing-rooms.*

Belinda   Dotty, my love!

Selsdon   Oh, she's emerged, has she? Come on, old girl! You're on!

Frederick   Are you all right?

Selsdon   Is she all right?

Dotty *merely sighs and smiles, and gives a little squeeze of the arm to* **Belinda**. *She takes up her place by the service quarters entrance, a tragically misunderstood woman.* **Garry** *moves pointedly away.*

Belinda (*to* **Selsdon**)   She's fine.

Tim   All right, everyone?

Selsdon   'Little hugs and squeezes.'

Belinda   Hush, love.

Poppy   Curtain up?

Everyone looks anxiously from **Dotty** *to* **Garry** *and back again.* **Dotty** *and* **Garry** *both ignore the looks. They stand aloof, then both at the same moment turn to check their appearance in the little mirrors fixed to the back of the set.*

Frederick   Look, Dotty . . . Look, Garry . . . I'm not going to make a great speech, but we *have* all got to go out there and put on a performance, and well . . .

Belinda   We can't do it in silence, my loves! We're going to have to speak to each other!

Pause. Neither **Garry** *nor* **Dotty** *has apparently heard.*

Dotty (*suddenly, bravely, to* **Tim**)   What's the house like?

Belinda   That's the spirit!

Frederick   Well done, Dotty!

Tim   It's quite good. Well, for a matinée.

Poppy   There's quite a crowd at the front of the back stalls.

Selsdon (*to* **Poppy**)   Come on, girl, get the tabs up! Some of those OAPs out there haven't got long to go.

Poppy   Right. Quiet, then, please . . .

Frederick   Let me just say one more word . . . Hold it a moment, Poppy . . .

Selsdon   Let *me* just say one word. Sardines!

Belinda   Sardines!

Frederick   Sardines!

Belinda *rushes to the prop table to fetch* **Dotty** *the plate of sardines that she takes on for her first entrance.*

Poppy (*over tannoy*)   Standing by, please. Music cue one . . .

Enter **Lloyd** *through the pass door.*

Lloyd   Now what?

Tim   We're just going up.

Lloyd   We've been sitting there for an hour! They've gone quiet! They think someone's died!

Frederick   I'm sorry, Lloyd. It's my fault. I was just saying a few words to everyone.

Lloyd   Freddie, have you ever thought of having a brain transplant?

Frederick   Sorry, sorry. Wrong moment. I see that.

Lloyd   Anybody else have thoughts they feel they must communicate?

Poppy   Well, not now, of course, but . . .

Lloyd   *What?*

Poppy   I mean, you know, later . . .

Lloyd (*to* **Tim**, *quietly, conscious that* **Brooke** *has stopped meditating and started watching*)   And you bought these flowers for Poppy?

Tim   No . . . (*Conscious that* **Poppy** *is watching.*) Well . . . yes . . .

Lloyd   And you didn't buy any flowers for *me*?

Tim   No . . . well . . . no . . .

Lloyd   Tim, have you ever heard of such a thing as jealous rage?

Tim   Yes . . . well . . . yes . . .

Lloyd   Then take ten pounds of your own money, Tim, and go out to the florists and buy some flowers for *me*!

Tim   Lloyd, we're just going up! I've got to run the show!

Lloyd   Never mind the show. Concentrate on the floral arrangements. Bought them for Poppy! You two could have Freddie's old brain. You could have half each.

Exit **Lloyd** *through the pass door.* **Poppy** *sobs.*

Frederick   Oh dear.

Belinda   Don't cry, Poppy, love

Selsdon   Just get the old bus on the road.

Poppy (*over tannoy, tearfully*)   Standing by, please. Elecs stand by.

Garry (*to himself*)   Christ! (*He hammers his fist against the back of the set in frustration.*)

Poppy   Quiet backstage!

She waits for **Garry** *to subside, then gives an involuntary noisy sob herself.*

Belinda   Hush, love.

Poppy (*over tannoy, tearfully*)   Music cue one go.

The introductory music for Nothing On.

Tabs going up . . .

[Note: the act that follows is a somewhat condensed version of the one we saw rehearsed.]

As the curtain rises the telephone is ringing.

Dotty makes her entrance.——

—— Enter from the service quarters **Mrs Clackett**, *carrying a plate of sardines.*

Mrs Clackett   It's no good you going on . . .

There is a sound of scattered applause. ——————————

—— She pauses a beat to acknowledge the applause.

I can't open sardines and answer the phone. I've only got one pair of feet.

A small laugh. ———————

————— Puts the sardines down on the telephone table by the sofa and picks up the phone.

Selsdon, Belinda *and* **Frederick** *express silent relief that the show has at last started, so all their problems are over. They subside on to the backstage chairs.*

Hello . . . Yes, but there's no one here, love . . . No, Mr Brent's not here . . . He lives here, yes, but he don't live here now because he lives in Spain . . . Mr Philip Brent, that's right . . . The one who writes the plays, that's him, only now he writes them in Spain . . . No, she's in Spain, too, they're all in Spain, there's no one here . . . Am I in Spain? No, I'm not in Spain, dear. I look after the house for them, but I go home at one o'clock on Wednesday, only I've got a nice plate of sardines to put my feet up with, because it's the royal what's it called on

Tim *puts his raincoat on, takes out his wallet, checks his money and exits to the dressing-rooms.*

Belinda *points out to the others that* **Garry** *is banging his head softly against the set again.*

Frederick *puts the whisky down on his chair and goes across to* **Garry**. **Belinda** *watches apprehensively as* **Frederick** *gives* **Garry**'s *arm a silently sympathetic squeeze, and smilingly puts his fingers to his lips to remind him to be quiet.*

the telly – the royal you know – where's the paper, then . . .

Belinda *hurries across to draw* **Frederick** *off.* **Frederick** *cannot understand what he has done to cause offence. He demonstrates what he did by giving* **Garry**'s *arm another friendly squeeze.*

Garry *drops his props and threatens to hit* **Frederick**.

She searches in the newspaper.

. . . And if it's to do with letting the house then you'll have to ring the house agents, because they're the agents for the house . . . Squire, Squire, Hackham and who's the other one . . . ? No, they're not in Spain, they're next to the phone in the study. Squire, Squire, Hackham and, hold on, I'll go and look.

She replaces the receiver.

Frederick *takes shelter behind* **Brooke**, *who is now waiting for her entrance.* **Garry** *chases him round and round her.*

Frederick *hurriedly puts his handkerchief to his nose.*

Belinda *urges* **Garry** *to the front door for his entrance.* ——————————

Always the same, isn't it. Soon as you take the weight off your feet, down it all comes on your head.

Exit **Mrs Clackett** *into the study, still holding the newspaper.*

The sound of a key in the lock.

—— *The front door opens. On the doorstep stands* **Roger**, *holding a cardboard box.*

Roger   . . . I have a housekeeper, yes, but this is her afternoon off.

Brooke *makes her entrance.* ——

—— *Enter* **Vicki** *through the front door.*

Frederick *looks in his handkerchief and comes over faint.* **Dotty** *has to put her arm round him to help him to a chair.*

As **Garry** *turns back ———— to collect the flight bag he gets a fleeting glimpse of this.*

As **Garry** *comes through the service quarters he takes another look. ————————————*

He stamps on **Frederick***'s foot and re-enters. ————————*

Frederick *struggles with damaged foot and bleeding nose.* **Dotty** *gets down on her knees to examine the foot.*

Garry *keeps appearing at the various doors, trying to see what* **Dotty** *and* **Frederick** *are up to. ————————————*

Belinda *makes things worse by trying to move* **Dotty***'s head to a less suggestive position.*

Roger   So we've got the place entirely to ourselves.

*———— * **Roger** *goes back and brings in a flight bag, and closes the front door.*

I'll just check.

———— He opens the door to the service quarters. **Vicki** *gazes round.*

Roger   Hello? Anyone at home?

———— Closes the door.

No, there's no one here. So what do you think?

Vicki   All these doors!

Roger   Oh, only a handful, really.

———— He opens the various doors one after another to demonstrate.

Study . . . Kitchen . . . And a self-contained service flat for the housekeeper.

Vicki   Terrific. And which one's the . . . ?

Roger   What?

Vicki   You know . . .

Garry *comes off* ———— *and rushes at* **Frederick** *and* **Dotty**. **Belinda** *pushes him back on stage.*

Belinda *just manages to detach* **Dotty** *from her ministrations and get her back on stage for her entrance.* ————

Belinda *tries to explain to* **Frederick** *that* **Dotty** *has taken a fancy to him.* **Frederick** *can't understand a word of it.*

Belinda *has to break off to remind* **Brooke** *to . . .*

. . . push the bathroom door open. ————————

Roger   The usual offices? Through here.

———— *He opens the downstairs bathroom door for her.*

Vicki   Fantastic.

Exit **Vicki** *into the bathroom.*

———— *Enter* **Mrs Clackett** *from the study, without the newspaper.*

Mrs Clackett   Now I've lost the sardines. . .

Mutual surprise. **Roger** *closes the door to the bathroom and slips the champagne back into the bag.*

Roger   I'm sorry. I thought there was no one here.

Mrs Clackett   I'm not here. I'm off, only it's the royal you know, where they wear those hats, and they're all covered in fruit, and who are you?

Roger   I'm from the agents. I just dropped in to . . . go into a few things.

———— *The bathroom door opens.*

Well, to check some of the measurements . . .

Roger *closes it.*

And again. ————————

———— *The bathroom door opens.*

Do one or two odd jobs . . .

Roger *closes it.*

Oh, and a client. I'm showing a prospective tenant over the house.

The bathroom door opens.

Belinda *suddenly points out that* **Selsdon** *has discovered the whisky that* **Frederick** *left on the chair.* **Selsdon** *opens the bottle, smells it, closes it again and then goes off to the dressing-rooms with it.*

Vicki What's wrong with this door?

Roger *closes it.*

Frederick *goes to run after* **Selsdon**. **Belinda** *silently urges him to wait there – sit still – do absolutely nothing – while she runs after* **Selsdon**.

Roger She's thinking of renting it. Her interest is definitely aroused.

Enter **Vicki** *from bathroom.*

Vicki That's not the bedroom.

Roger The bedroom? No, that's the downstairs bathroom and WC suite. And this is the housekeeper, Mrs Crockett.

Exit **Belinda** *in the direction of the dressing-rooms in pursuit of* **Selsdon**.

Mrs Clackett Clackett, dear, Clackett. Only now I've lost the newspaper.

———— *Exit* **Mrs Clackett** *into the study, carrying the sardines.*

Dotty *makes her exit . . .* —— *puts down the sardines, shaking her head with misery, and begins to weep.*

Roger I'm sorry about this.

Frederick is very agitated by this. He takes the sardines away from **Dotty***, pats her on the shoulder, gives her a handkerchief, realises that it's not in a state to be seen, puts it hurriedly away, pushes the sardines back into her hand and edges her towards the door.*

Vicki   That's all right. We don't want the television, do we?

Roger   Only she's been in the family for generations.

Vicki   Great. Come on, then. (*She starts upstairs.*) I've got to be in Basingstoke by four.

Roger   Perhaps we should just have a glass of champagne.

Vicki   We'll take it up with us.

Roger   Yes. Well . . .

Vicki   And don't let my files out of sight.

Roger   No. Only . . .

Vicki   What?

Roger   Well . . .

Vicki   Her?

At the last moment **Dotty** *realises she hasn't got the newspaper.*

Frederick *runs and fetches it from the props table.* **Dotty** *realises that she is still holding the sardines, and hurls them to* **Frederick** *just in time . . .*

Roger   She *has* been in the family for generations.

. . . to make her entrance.——

——— Enter **Mrs Clackett** *from the study, with the newspaper but without the sardines.*

Enter **Belinda** *from the dressing-rooms leading a bewildered* **Selsdon**, *but without the whisky.*

Mrs Clackett   Sardines . . . Sardines . . . It's not for me to say, of course, dear, only I will just say this: don't think twice about it – take the plunge. You'll really enjoy it here.

Vicki   Oh. Great.

Frederick *tells her what a terrible state* **Dotty** *is in.*

Mrs Clackett (*to* **Vicki**) And we'll enjoy having you. (*To* **Roger**.) Won't we, love?

Roger   Oh. Well.

Vicki   Terrific.

Mrs Clackett   Sardines, sardines. Can't put your feet up on an empty stomach, can you.

They turn to watch her anxiously as she makes her exit. ————

—— *Exit* **Mrs Clackett** *to service quarters.*

Vicki   You see? She thinks it's great. She's even making us sardines!

Selsdon *seizes the opportunity to depart again to the dressing-rooms.*

Roger   Well. . .

Vicki   I think she's terrific.

Belinda *runs after* **Selsdon**. **Frederick** *goes to run after her, but turns anxiously back to reassure* **Dotty**.

Roger   Terrific.

Vicki   So which way?

Roger (*picking up the bags*) All right. Before she comes back with the sardines.

But **Dotty** *is now smiling bravely and telling* **Frederick** *that she has pulled herself together, thanks to him.*

Vicki   Up here?

Roger   Yes, yes.

Dotty *gives* **Frederick** *a kiss to express her gratitude.*

As **Garry** *comes through* —— *the door of the mezzanine bathroom he catches a fleeting glimpse of the kiss.*

Frederick *takes the cardboard box and goes to make his entrance, then turns back to pick up the flight bag and looks round for* **Belinda** *to give it to. No* **Belinda**. *He urgently shows* **Dotty** *the flight bag and explains the situation to her.*

Garry *appears in the linen cupboard doorway.* ——— *He takes a good look at the earnest colloquy between* **Frederick** *and* **Dotty**.

Garry *takes the sheet from* **Brooke**. ———————

Garry *hurls the sheet at* **Frederick** *and* **Dotty**. —— *He goes back on stage.*

Dotty *starts to run off to get* **Belinda**, *but has to run back to help* **Frederick**.

Vicki   In here?

Roger   Yes, yes, yes.

—— *Exeunt* **Roger** *and* **Vicki** *into mezzanine bathroom.*

Vicki (*off*)   It's another bathroom.

They reappear.

Roger   No, no, no.

Vicki   Always trying to get me into bathrooms.

Roger   I mean in *here*.

He nods at the next door – the first along the gallery. **Vicki** *leads the way in.*

—— **Roger** *follows.*

Vicki   Oh, black sheets!

—— *She produces one.*

Roger   It's the airing cupboard.

—— This one, this one.

He drops the bag and box, and struggles nervously to open the second door along the gallery, the bedroom.

Vicki   Oh, you're in a real state! You can't even get the door open.

Belinda runs in from the dressing-room, holding the bottle of whisky.

She grabs the flight bag, just manages to give the whisky to **Dotty***, and . . .*

. . . make her entrance. ⸺

Enter **Selsdon** *from the dressing-rooms.*

He asks **Dotty** *for the whisky.*

But **Dotty** *is distracted by* **Garry***, who silently but forcefully explains to her that he will no longer tolerate these furtive meetings with* **Frederick***.*

Selsdon tries urgently to get the whisky off **Garry** *and* **Dotty** *as they quarrel.*

Garry *and* **Dotty** *both turn on him in fury.*

Garry *pleads with* **Dotty** –

Exeunt **Roger** *and* **Vicki** *into the bedroom.*

The sound of a key in the lock and the front door opens. On the doorstep stands **Philip***, carrying a cardboard box.*

Philip   . . . No, it's Mrs Clackett's afternoon off, remember.

⸺ *Enter* **Flavia***, carrying a flight bag like* **Roger***'s.*

Flavia   Home!

Philip   Home, sweet home!

Flavia   Dear old house!

Philip   Just waiting for us to come back!

Flavia   It's rather funny, though, creeping in like this for our wedding anniversary!

Philip *picks up the bag and box and ushers* **Flavia** *towards the stairs.*

Philip   There is something to be said for being a tax exile.

Flavia   Leave those!

He drops the bag and box, and kisses her. She flees upstairs, laughing, and he after her.

Philip   Sh!

kneels – weeps – hangs on to her plate of sardines.

Dotty *breaks away from* **Garry** *and goes to makes her entrance.* **Selsdon** *points out that she is still holding the whisky.*

Garry *takes it off her as she makes her entrance.* ————

Selsdon *tries to get the whisky off* **Garry***, but* **Garry** *turns to ascend the platform for his entrance.*

Garry *looks around for something to do with the whisky and gives it to* **Brooke***.*

Brooke *peers at it, no idea what she's supposed to do with it.*

She puts it down on the steps, right in front of **Selsdon***, in order to undress for her entrance. While her back is turned* **Selsdon** *snatches it up and conceals it.*

Flavia   What?

Philip   Inland Revenue may hear us!

They creep to the bedroom door.

———— *Enter* **Mrs Clackett** *from the service quarters carrying a fresh plate of sardines.*

Mrs Clackett (*to herself*) What I did with that first lot of sardines I shall never know.

She puts the sardines on the telephone table and sits on the sofa.

Philip *and* **Flavia** (*looking down from the gallery*)   Mrs Clackett!

Mrs Clackett *jumps up.*

Mrs Clackett   Oh, you give me a turn! My heart jumped right out of my boots!

Philip   So did mine!

Flavia   We thought you'd gone!

Mrs Clackett   I thought you was in Spain!

Philip   We are! We are!

Flavia You haven't seen us!

Selsdon *demonstrates to* **Brooke** *pulling a chain.* **Brooke** *peers uncomprehendingly.*

Philip We're not here!

Mrs Clackett You'll want your things, look. (*She indicates the bag and box.*)

Philip Oh. Yes. Thanks.

He comes downstairs, and picks up the bag and box.

Exit **Selsdon** *to the dressing-rooms with the whisky.*

Mrs Clackett (*to* **Flavia**) Oh, and that bed hasn't been aired, love.

Flavia I'll get a hot-water bottle.

Belinda *makes her exit.* ——

—— *Exit* **Flavia** *into the mezzanine bathroom.*

Mrs Clackett I've put all your letters in the study, dear.

Belinda *looks urgently round for* **Selsdon**, *then makes drinking gestures interrogatively to* **Brooke**. **Brooke** *points towards the dressing-rooms and repeats* **Selsdon**'s *incomprehensible gesture of pulling a chain. Exit* **Belinda** *towards the dressing-room.*

Philip Oh, good heavens. Where are they?

Mrs Clackett I've put them all in the pigeonhouse.

Philip In the pigeonhouse?

Mrs Clackett In the little pigeonhouse in your desk, love.

Garry, *still on the platform, tries to see what* **Dotty** *and* **Frederick** *are doing, but is fetched back by* **Brooke** . . .

Exeunt **Mrs Clackett** *and* **Philip** *into the study.* **Philip** *is still holding the bag and box.*

. . . for his entrance. ——————

Belinda enters urgently and signals the information that Selsdon is drinking in the lavatory.

Frederick runs to the dressing-rooms exit to deal with this, but is brought back by Belinda and forced to sit down.

Dotty and Belinda run towards the dressing-rooms instead, but Dotty immediately has to run back to the study door to go on. Belinda runs back to the props table for the sardines, gives them to Dotty, just in time for her . . .

. . . to make her entrance. ——————

—— *Enter* **Roger** *from the bedroom, still dressed, tying his tie.*

Roger   Yes, but I could hear voices!

Enter **Vicki** *from the bedroom in her underwear.*

Vicki   Voices? What sort of voices?

Roger   People's voices.

Vicki (*looks over the bannisters*) Oh, look, she's opened our sardines.

She moves to go downstairs. **Roger** *grabs her.*

Roger   Come back!

Vicki   What?

Roger   I'll fetch them! You can't go downstairs like that.

Vicki   Why not?

Roger   Mrs Crackett.

Vicki   Mrs Crackett?

Roger   One has certain obligations.

—— *Enter* **Mrs Clackett** *from the study. She is carrying the first plate of sardines.*

Mrs Clackett (*to herself*) Sardines here. Sardines

there. It's like a Sunday school outing.

—— **Roger** *pushes* **Vicki** *through the first available door, which happens to be the linen cupboard.*

Brooke *makes her exit.* ——

Mrs Clackett   Oh, you're still poking around, are you?

Belinda *tries to demonstrate to* **Brooke** *that she is going to look for* **Selsdon**, *then runs back to remind her . . .*

Roger   Yes, still poking . . . well, still around.

Mrs Clackett   In the airing cupboard, were you?

Roger   No, no.

. . . to open the linen cupboard door. ——————

—— *The linen cupboard door begins to open. He slams it shut.*

Well, just checking the sheets and pillowcases. Going through the inventory.

Enter **Tim** *from the dressing-rooms with a second, smaller, bunch of flowers. He takes his raincoat off.* **Belinda** *gestures hastily to* **Tim** *in passing to explain the situation and exits to the dressing-rooms.*

He starts downstairs.

Mrs Blackett . . .

Mrs Clackett   Clackett, dear, Clackett.

She puts down the sardines beside the other sardines.

Tim *asks* **Frederick** *where she is going.*

Frederick *demonstrates raising the elbow.*

Roger   Mrs Clackett. Is there anyone else in the house, Mrs Clackett?

Enter **Belinda** *from the dressing-rooms. She demonstrates that* **Selsdon** *has locked himself in somewhere.*

Mrs Clackett   I haven't seen no one, dear.

Frederick *breaks off from the conversation to say* —————

Tim *hands* **Belinda** *the flowers and dashes out to the dressing-rooms.*

Belinda *gives the flowers to* **Frederick** *and fetches the fireman's axe from the fire-point. She demonstrates using it to break a door down.*

Belinda *is going to rush off to the dressing-rooms with the axe when* **Poppy** *reminds her that she has an entrance coming up.* **Belinda** *runs up on to the platform, finds that she is still holding the axe and gives it to* **Brooke**.

But before **Belinda** *can explain what to do with the axe, she has to make her entrance.* —————

Garry *advances threateningly upon* **Frederick** *and points suspiciously at the flowers he is holding.*

Roger   I thought I heard voices.

Mrs Clackett   Voices? There's no voices here, love.

Roger   I must have imagined it.

—— **Philip** (*off*)   Oh, good Lord above!

Roger, *with his back to her, picks up both plates of sardines.*

Roger   I beg your pardon?

Mrs Clackett   Oh, good Lord above, the study door's open.

She crosses and closes it. **Roger** *looks out of the window.*

Roger   There's another car outside! That's not Mr Hackham's, is it? Or Mr Dudley's?

Exit **Roger** *through the front door, holding both plates of sardines.*

—— *Enter* **Flavia** *from the mezzanine bathroom, carrying a hot-water bottle. She sees the linen cupboard door swinging open as she passes, pushes it shut and turns the key.*

Flavia   Nothing but flapping doors in this house.

Frederick *has to hand* **Garry** *the flowers in order to make his entrance.*————

Brooke *comes down from the platform and asks* **Garry** *what she is supposed to do with the axe.* **Garry** *takes it thoughtfully and puts the flowers into her hands.* **Belinda**, *coming down from the platform to go off after* **Selsdon**, *stops at the sight of* **Garry** *with the axe, as he looks at it and feels the edge. He looks at the door through which* **Frederick** *will exit.* **Belinda** *looks at the door likewise.* **Garry** *looks back at the axe.* **Belinda** *looks back at the axe.* **Garry** *begins to smile an evil smile. Horrified,* **Belinda** *quickly takes the flowers from* **Brooke** *and sends her off in her place to find* **Selsdon**, *then tries to get the axe away from* **Garry**. **Garry** *holds it behind his back.* **Belinda**, *still holding the flowers, puts her arms round* **Garry**, *trying to reach the axe.*

Dotty *appears*———— *just in time to see* **Belinda** *with her arms round* **Garry**.

Poppy *urges* **Belinda** *upstairs for her entrance.* **Belinda** *flees up to the platform and opens the door to make her entrance.*————

Exit **Flavia** *into the bedroom.*

———— *Enter from the study* **Philip**, *holding a tax demand and its envelope.*

Philip   '. . . final notice . . . steps will be taken . . . distraint . . . proceedings in court . . .'

Mrs Clackett   Oh yes, and that reminds me, a gentleman come about the house.

Philip   Don't tell me. I'm not here.

Mrs Clackett   So I'll just sit down and turn on the . . . sardines, I've forgotten the sardines! I don't know – if it wasn't fixed to my shoulders I'd forget what day it was.

———— *Exit* **Mrs Clackett** *to the service quarters.*

Philip   I didn't get this! I'm not here. I'm in Spain. But if I didn't get it I didn't open it.

———— *Enter* **Flavia** *from the bedroom.*

She makes one desperate effort to grab the dress from the backstage hook where it is hanging, then gives up, and enters still carrying the flowers instead.——————

—— She is holding the dress that **Vicki** *arrived in.*

Flavia   Darling, I never had a dress . . .

Belinda, *on stage, has to vary the line.* ——————————

—— . . . or rather a bunch of flowers like this, did I?

Dotty *launches herself upon* **Garry**. *He produces the axe in explanation of his behaviour.* **Dotty** *snatches it from him and raises it to hit him.*

Philip (*abstracted*)   Didn't you?

Flavia   I shouldn't buy anything as tarty as this . . . Oh, it's not something you gave me, is it?

Philip   I should never have touched it.

Flavia   No, it's lovely.

Philip   Stick it down. Put it back. Never saw it.

Frederick *appears* —————— *and snatches the axe from* **Dotty**, *in the nick of time. He innocently gives it to* **Garry**, *who raises it to hit* **Frederick**. **Dotty** *snatches it from* **Garry** *and raises it once again to hit him.*

—— Exit **Philip** *into study.*

Flavia   Well, I'll put it in the attic, with all the other things you gave me that are too precious to wear.

Belinda *appears* —————— *and snatches the axe from* **Dotty**. . .

—— Exit **Flavia** *along the upstairs corridor.*

. . . *as* **Garry** *makes his entrance.*————————

————— *Enter* **Roger** *through the front door, still carrying both plates of sardines.*

Roger   All right, all right . . . Now the study door's open again! What's going on?

Enter **Tim** *from the dressing-rooms. He grabs the axe from* **Belinda** *and returns to the dressing-rooms.*

He puts the sardines down – one plate on the telephone table, where it was before, one near the front door – and goes towards the study . . .

Belinda *is going to follow him, but then realises that there is . . .*

. . . *no knocking* ——————— *because* **Brooke** *is still off.*

————— Knocking!

Garry *on stage repeats the line.* ———————

————— Knocking . . . ! Knocking . . . ? Upstairs!

Belinda *realises what's wrong, and knocks on the set with a prop.*————————

He runs upstairs.

————— *Knocking.*

Oh my God, there's something in the airing cupboard! (*He unlocks it and opens it.*)

Brooke *doesn't make* ——— *her entrance because she is still off in the dressing-rooms.*

————— *Looks for* **Vicki**.

Garry *comes through the linen cupboard door to look for* **Brooke**.

Oh, it's you.

He improvises. ———————

Belinda *tells* **Poppy** *to read in* **Brooke**'s *part from the book.*

————— Is it you . . . ? I mean, you know, hidden under all the sheets and towels in

Belinda *hands the flowers to* **Frederick** *and runs off to the dressing-rooms, still holding the axe.*

Poppy (*reading*)   Of course it's me! You put me in here! In the dark! With all black sheets and things! —————

Why did *I* lock the door? Why did *you* lock the door! –

Enter **Lloyd** *like a whirlwind through the pass door. He demands silently to know what's going on.* **Frederick** *tries to explain, while* **Poppy** *and* **Garry** *continue to play the scene.*

Poppy (*reading*)   *Someone* locked the door!—————

Frederick *hands* **Lloyd** *the flowers to make ready for his entrance.*

Poppy (*reading*)   Like what?

OK, I'll take it off.—————

Lloyd *shoves the flowers into* **Dotty**'s *hands to get rid of them, and indicates to the terrified* **Poppy** *that she is to go on for* **Brooke**.

here . . . I can't just stand here and, you know, indefinitely . . .

—————

Roger   But, darling, why did you lock the door?

—————

Roger   I didn't lock the door!

—————

Roger   Anyway, we can't stand here like this.

—————

Roger   In your underwear.

—————

Roger   In here, in here!

Exit **Roger** *into the bedroom.*

Enter **Philip** *from the study, holding the tax demand, the envelope, and a tube of glue.*

Enter **Belinda** *from the dressing-rooms with* **Brooke**, *just in time for her to see* **Lloyd** *tearing* **Poppy**'s *skirt off.*

Garry *stands half on and half off, waiting for* **Brooke**. ——— *At the sight of* **Brooke**, **Lloyd** *abandons* **Poppy**, *and instead urges* **Brooke** *upstairs for the next scene, for which she is now late.*

Garry *improvises.* ———

Brooke *makes her entrance through the linen cupboard door . . .*

. . . and starts to play the previous scene that she missed. ———

Lloyd *despairs at* **Brooke**'s *inflexibility.* **Dotty** *asks* **Lloyd** *if the flowers are really for her. He pushes them back to her absently.* **Dotty** *is very touched. She gives* **Lloyd** *a grateful kiss . . .*

. . . just as **Garry** *appears to see it.*———————

Philip   Darling, this glue. Is it the sort that you can never get unstuck . . . ? Oh, Mrs Clackett's made us some sardines.

Exit **Philip** *into the study with the tax demand, envelope, glue and one of the plates of sardines from the telephone table.*

——— *Enter* **Roger** *from the bedroom, holding the hot-water bottle. He looks up and down the landing.*

Roger   A hot-water bottle! I didn't put it there!

——— I didn't put this hot-water bottle. I mean, you know, I'm standing out here, with the hot-water bottle in my hands . . .

———**Vicki**   Of course it's me! You put me in here! In the dark! With all black sheets and things!

Roger   Someone in the bathroom, filling hot-water bottles. . . What?

——— *Exit* **Roger** *into the mezzanine bathroom.*

Garry *moves closer to see, and cuts three pages of script.*————

He panics and stands for a moment, unable to think where he is or what he is doing, then enters through the airing cupboard instead of the bedroom. Everyone backstage panics as well: 'Where are we?'

Poppy *desperately turns over the pages of the book to find the new place, while* **Garry** *and everyone else look over her shoulder.*

Enter **Tim** *from the dressing-rooms, leading* **Selsdon***, who is holding his trousers up.* **Tim** *is holding the whisky and the axe embedded in a shattered section of the door of the Gents. He hands the whisky to* **Frederick***.*

Frederick *roars with surprise,* ———————— *claps a hand over his mouth, then realises that he was supposed to roar anyway.*

With another cry **Frederick** *hastily conceals the whisky under*

Vicki   Why did *I* lock the door? Why did *you* lock the door!

———— **Roger** *(off)*   Don't panic!

Enter **Roger***, and goes downstairs.*

There's some perfectly rational explanation for all this. I'll fetch Mrs Splotchett and she'll tell us what's happening. You wait here . . . You can't stand here looking like that . . . Wait in the study . . . Study, study, study!

Exit **Roger** *into the service quarters.*

Vicki *opens the study door.*

———— *There's a roar of exasperation from* **Philip***, off. She turns and flees.*

Vicki   Roger! There's a strange figure in there! Where are you?

There is another cry from **Philip***, off.*

*the chairs, grabs his props
and . . .*

. . . makes his entrance. ———

Tim *gives the axe to* **Lloyd**
and snatches the flowers from
Dotty*, who snatches them right
back, leaving* **Tim** *with only
one. He hands this to* **Lloyd***,
who hands it to* **Brooke***. She
peers at it as it keels sadly over,
then hurls it on to the floor and
runs out to the dressing-rooms.*

Lloyd *gives more money to*
Tim*, who puts his raincoat on
and exits wearily to the dressing-
rooms.*

Selsdon *explains to everyone
where he innocently was by a
show of pulling a chain. The
demonstration causes his trousers
to fall down.* **Selsdon** *stoops to
retrieve his fallen trousers, and
sees the whisky that* **Frederick**
concealed beneath the chairs. He

Exit **Vicki** *blindly through the
front door.*

——— *Enter* **Philip** *from the
study. He is holding the tax
demand in his right hand and
one of the plates of sardines in his
left.*

Philip   Darling, I know
this is going to sound silly,
but . . .

*He struggles to get the tax demand
unstuck from his fingers,
encumbered by the plate of
sardines.*

Enter **Flavia** *along the upstairs
corridor, carrying various pieces of
bric-a-brac.*

Flavia   Darling, if we're
not going to bed I'm going
to clear out the attic.

Philip   I can't come to
bed! I'm glued to a tax
demand!

Flavia   Darling, why don't
you put the sardines down?

Philip *puts the plate of sardines
down on the table. But when he
takes his hand away the sardines
come with it.*

Philip   Darling, I'm stuck
to the sardines!

Flavia   Darling, don't play
the fool. Get that bottle

picks it up, and **Lloyd** *snatches it out of his hand.*

Frederick *exits——————— and sees that* **Selsdon** *is otherwise occupied.*

Frederick *repeats the cue —— and slams the door again.*

They all suddenly realise that this is **Selsdon**'s *cue. They rush him to the window. He raises his arms to open the window and his trousers fall down.*

They bundle him on as best they can.——————————————

They watch him. Then **Garry** *snatches the flowers from* **Dotty**, *and hurls them on the floor.* **Frederick** *reproachfully picks them up, and hands them back to* **Dotty**.

Garry *grabs the axe from* **Lloyd** *and advances upon* **Frederick**. **Dotty** *hands the*

marked poison in the downstairs loo. That eats through anything.

Exit **Flavia** *along the upstairs corridor.*

Philip (*flapping the tax demand*)   I've heard of people getting stuck with a problem, but this is ridiculous.

—— Exit **Philip** *into the downstairs bathroom.*

—— **Philip**   But this is ridiculous.

Exit **Philip** *into the downstairs bathroom.*

—— The window opens, and through it appears an elderly **Burglar**.

Burglar   No bars, no burglar alarm. They ought to be prosecuted for incitement.

He climbs in.

No, but sometimes it makes me want to sit down and weep. When I think I used to do banks! When I remember I used to do *flowers to* **Belinda** *so as to be able to throw her arms protectively round* **Frederick**. **Belinda** *dumps the flowers on* **Poppy**'s *desk so as to be able to snatch* **Frederick** *away from* **Dotty**. **Dotty** *snatches him back. They snatch him back and forth, like two dogs with a bone, then push him aside and face up to each other.* **Dotty** *grabs the axe from* **Garry** *to use on* **Belinda**. *But they are distracted because . . .*

bullion vaults! What am I doing now? I'm breaking into paper bags! So what are they offering? (*He peers at the television.*) One microwave oven.

He unplugs it and puts it on the sofa.

What? Fifty quid? Hardly worth lifting it.

He inspects the paintings and ornaments.

Junk . . . Junk . . . if you insist . . .

He pockets some small item.

Selsdon *appears at the front door.* ——————————

Where's his desk? No, they all say the same thing . . .

Selsdon   Yes? Yes? 'They all say the same thing . . . ?'

—— *He opens the front door to get a prompt.*

Poppy *runs back with the flowers to the corner to give him his prompt.*

Poppy   'It's hard to adjust to retirement.'

Selsdon   Hard to what?

Omnes (*shouting*) 'Adjust to retirement!'

Selsdon *goes back on.*————

——It's hard to assess a requirement . . .

Selsdon *makes his exit.*————

—— *Exit* **Burglar** *into the study.*

Dotty *is about to resume her attack upon* **Belinda** *when she realises that* **Garry** *is already making his entrance.*————

Dotty *hands the axe panic-stricken to* **Belinda** *and makes her own entrance.*————

Lloyd *subsides despairingly into a chair.*

Frederick *indicates that he will go after* **Brooke**.
Belinda *insists that she will do it. She runs towards the dressing-rooms with the axe, sees* **Lloyd** *taking a despairing swig of whisky, and runs back to take the bottle away from him.*

Frederick *smoothes his hair and buttons his jacket, and exits with determination towards the dressing-rooms.*

Belinda *looks to see how much* **Lloyd** *has drunk, puts it out of his reach, runs towards the dressing-rooms, realises* **Selsdon** *has picked up the whisky, and runs back.*

———— *Enter* **Roger** *from the service quarters.*

Roger   . . . And the prospective tenant naturally wishes to know if there is any previous history of paranormal phenomena.

———— *Enter* **Mrs Clackett**, *holding another plate of sardines.*

Mrs Clackett   Oh, yes, dear, it's all nice and paranormal.

Roger   I mean, has anything ever dematerialised before? Has anything ever . . .

He sees the television set on the sofa.

. . . flown about?

Mrs Clackett *puts the sardines down on the telephone table, moves the television set back, and closes the front door.*

Mrs Clackett   Flown about? No, the things move themselves on their own two feet, just like they do in any house.

Enter **Tim** *from the dressing-rooms with a third, very small bunch of flowers. He gives them to* **Lloyd**, *but* **Belinda** *shows* **Lloyd Selsdon** *concealing the whisky about his person and* **Lloyd** *goes to deal with him, then comes back to give* **Belinda** *the flowers so as to leave his hands free.* **Selsdon** *quickly conceals the whisky in the fire-bucket.*

Lloyd *searches* **Selsdon**. ——

Selsdon *demonstrates that his hands are empty.*

Belinda *hands the axe to* **Tim** *and gives* **Lloyd** *a grateful kiss for the flowers.*

Enter **Frederick** *triumphantly from the dressing-rooms, bringing a reluctant* **Brooke** *back, still in her overcoat and carrying the holdall.*

She reluctantly starts to take the overcoat off, then peers at the spectacle of **Belinda**, *with flowers, kissing* **Lloyd**.

Tim, *seeing this as he takes his raincoat off, puts the raincoat back on again, hands the axe to* **Lloyd** *and wearily holds out his hand for money.*

Roger   I'd better warn the prospective tenant. She is inspecting the study.

He opens the study door and then closes it again.

There's a man in there!

Mrs Clackett   No, no, there's no one in the house, love.

Roger   (*opening the study door*) Look! Look!

—— He's . . . *searching for something.*

Mrs Clackett (*glancing briefly*)   I can't see no one.

Roger   You can't see him? But this is extraordinary! And where is my prospective tenant? I left her in there! She's gone! My prospective tenant has disappeared!

He closes the study door and looks round the living-room. He sees the sardines on the telephone table.

Oh my God.

Mrs Clackett Now what?

Roger   There!

Mrs Clackett   Where?

Roger   The sardines!

Lloyd *wearily hands the axe to* **Frederick** *and gives* **Tim** *his last small change.*

Exit **Tim** *to the dressing-rooms.* **Belinda** *suddenly realises that her flowers are attracting jealous attention and puts them on* **Poppy**'s *table with the other flowers.*

Brooke *is amazed and even more upset to see that the flowers are in fact for* **Poppy**. *She puts her overcoat back on and turns to walk out again.*

Lloyd *stops her and looks desperately round for some other token of his affection to give her instead of the flowers.*

Frederick, *tidily putting the axe back on the fire point, finds the whisky in the fire-bucket and holds it aloft – another bottle!*

Selsdon *takes the bottle from* **Frederick**, *but* **Lloyd** *takes it from* **Selsdon** *in time for. . .*

. . . **Selsdon** *to make his entrance.*————————

Lloyd *gives the whisky to* **Brooke**, *kisses her, and tries to persuade her out of her overcoat, while she peers at the bottle.*

Mrs Clackett   Oh, the sardines.

Roger   You can see the sardines.

Mrs Clackett   I can see the sardines.

Roger *touches them cautiously, then picks up the plate.*

Mrs Clackett   I can see the way they're going, too.

Roger   I'm not letting these sardines out of my hand. But where is my prospective tenant?

He goes upstairs, holding the sardines.

Mrs Clackett   I'm going to be opening sardines all night, in and out of here like a cuckoo on a clock.

Exit **Mrs Clackett** *into the service quarters.*

Roger   Vicki! Vicki!

Exit **Roger** *into the mezzanine bathroom.*

———— *Enter* **Burglar** *from the study, carrying an armful of silver cups, etc.*

Burglar   No, I miss the violence. I miss having other human beings around to terrify.

Frederick *takes the whisky out of* **Brooke***'s hands.*

Lloyd *takes it back and hands it to* **Brooke***.* **Frederick** *takes it away again to show it to* **Dotty***, turning her round to show that it came from the fire bucket, just as . . .*

. . . **Garry** *makes his exit and sees* **Dotty** *now apparently being hugged by* **Frederick***.———*

Garry *leans down from the platform and tips the plate of sardines he is carrying over* **Dotty***'s head. Everyone, even* **Brooke***, half in and half out of her coat, watches, hands helplessly upraised.*

Garry *makes his entrance. ——*

Dotty *puts the whisky down on the steps to deal with the sardines on her head.*

Garry *makes his exit ——— then picks up the whisky and takes a swig, very pleased with himself.*

While **Garry** *stands on the platform with his head back,* **Dotty** *climbs on a chair and ties his shoelaces together.*

He dumps the silverware on the sofa and exits into the study.

Enter **Roger** *from mezzanine bathroom.*

Roger   Where's she gone? Vicki?

—— Exit **Roger** *into the bedroom.*

Enter **Burglar** *from the study, carrying* **Philip***'s box and bag. He empties the contents of the box out behind the sofa and loads the silverware into the box.*

Burglar   It's nice to hear a bit of shouting and screaming around you. All this silence gets you down.

—— Enter **Roger** *from the linen cupboard, still holding the sardines.*

Roger (*calls*)   Vicki! Vicki!

—— Exit **Roger** *into the bedroom.*

Burglar   I'm going to end up talking to myself . . .

Exit the **Burglar** *into study, unaware of* **Roger***.*

Enter **Philip** *from the downstairs bathroom. His right*

Everyone, even **Brooke***, watches, horrified.*

Lloyd *tries to warn* **Garry***.* **Garry** *brushes him aside because he has an entrance coming up.*

Garry *puts the whisky down and . . .*

makes his entrance ——————— *falling headlong over his feet.*

Dotty *demonstrates to* **Belinda** *and* **Lloyd** *what she did, half delighted and half shocked at herself.*

Everyone tries to see what's happening on stage, also half delighted and half shocked.

hand is still stuck to the tax demand, his left to the plate of sardines.

Philip   Darling, this stuff that eats through anything. It eats through *trousers!*

He examines holes burnt in the front of them.

Darling, if it eats through trousers, you don't think it goes on and eats through. . . Listen, darling, I think I'd better get these trousers off! (*He begins to do so, as best he can.*) Darling, I think I can feel it! I think it's eating through . . . absolutely everything!

—— *Enter* **Roger** *from the bedroom, still holding the sardines.*

Roger   There's something evil in this house.

Philip *pulls up his trousers.*

Philip (*aside*)   The Inland Revenue!

Roger (*sees* **Philip***, frightened*)   He's back!

Philip   I must go.

Roger   Stay!

Philip   I won't, thank you.

Selsdon *finds the bottle on the platform – yet another bottle!*

Lloyd *takes the whisky away from* **Selsdon** *mechanically.*

Lloyd, **Dotty**, *and* **Belinda** *all take swigs from it in turns, absent-mindedly, as they follow events on stage.*

Dotty *holds up her hand to get attention to the events on stage. She demonstrates that* **Garry** *is going to have to run downstairs.*

They all wait for the crash.

The sound of **Garry** *falling downstairs.————————*

Even **Selsdon** *can hear it.*

No sound from the stage. Everyone listens and as they listen the laughter dies away.

Roger   Speak!

Philip   Only in the presence of my lawyer.

Roger   Only in the presence of your . . . ? Hold on. You're not from the other world!

Philip   Yes, yes – Marbella!

Roger   You're some kind of intruder!

Philip   Well, nice to meet you.

He waves goodbye with his right hand, then sees the tax demand on it and hurriedly puts it away behind his back.

I mean, have a sardine.

He offers the sardines on his left hand. His trousers, unsupported, fall down.

Roger   No, you're not! You're some kind of sex maniac! You've done something to Vicki! I'm going to come straight downstairs . . .

—— **Roger** *falls downstairs.*

Frederick, *on stage,*
improvises a line.————

No reply.

Belinda *turns to* **Dotty** *in*
horror – she's killed him!
Belinda *opens the study door to*
go to **Garry**. **Lloyd** *restrains*
her.

At the sound of **Garry**'s
voice ————————————
they all relax.

Lloyd *takes another swig of*
whisky.

Frederick *makes his exit,*————
trousers round his ankles,
handkerchief pressed to his nose.
He looks into his handkerchief
and comes over faint. **Belinda**
and **Dotty** *catch him.*

Lloyd *remembers that*
Brooke *has an entrance coming*
up. He attempts to peel the
overcoat off her.

Brooke, *recoiling from this,*
reverses into **Belinda** *and*
Dotty, *staggering under the*
weight of **Frederick**, *and loses*
her lenses.

Belinda *and* **Dotty** *drop*
Frederick *and turn to deal*
with this next problem.

Garry *repeats the cue.* ————

———**Philip**   Are you all
right?

———**Roger** (*faintly*)   This
is plainly a matter for the
police. (*Into the phone.*) Police!

Philip   I think I'll be
running along.

——— *He runs, his trousers still*
round his ankles, out through the
front door.

Roger   Come back . . . !
(*Into the phone.*) Hello . . .
police? Someone has broken
into my house! Or rather
someone has broken into
someone's house . . . No, but
he's a sex maniac! I left a
young woman here and
what's happened to her no
one knows!

——— And what's happened
to her no one *knows*!

Garry *appears, still hobbled, in the study doorway, and furiously repeats the cue yet again.* ——

—— No one *knows!*

Belinda, **Dotty** *and* **Lloyd** *guide* **Brooke**, *blinded and confused, and still wearing her overcoat, to the window for her entrance, cracking her head against the set on the way.*——

—— *Enter* **Vicki** *through the window.*

They watch as **Brooke** *falls headlong over the sofa on stage.*

Vicki   There's a man lurking in the undergrowth!

Roger (*into the phone*) Sorry . . . the young woman has reappeared. (*Hand over phone.*) Are you all right?

Vicki   No, he almost saw me!

Selsdon *suggests to* **Dotty** *that the lenses may be in her clothes.*

Roger (*into the phone*)   He almost saw her . . . Yes, but he's a burglar as well! He's taken our things!

Vicki (*finds* **Philip***'s bag and box*)   The things are here.

Roger (*into the phone*)   So what am I saying? I'm saying, let's say no more about it. (*He puts the phone down.*) Well, put something on!

Selsdon *searches* **Dotty***'s clothes. She can't understand what he's after.*

Vicki   I haven't got anything!

Roger   There must be something in the bathroom!

He picks up the box and bag, and leads the way.

Bring the sardines!

She picks up the sardines.

Garry *comes hobbling and raging off,——— his shoes still tied together. He gazes in amazement at the sight of* **Dotty** *and* **Selsdon**.

——— *Exeunt* **Roger** *and* **Vicki** *into the downstairs bathroom.*

Garry *repeats the cue.* ———

——— Bring the sardines!

Lloyd *realises and rushes* **Selsdon** *on, as* **Frederick** *loads him with props.*———

——— *Enter the* **Burglar** *from the study and dumps more booty.*

Garry *moves to commit violence upon everyone in sight, but the state of his shoes prevents him from getting more than a step or two before he has to return . . .*

Burglar   Right, that's downstairs tidied up a bit. (*He starts upstairs.*) Just give the upstairs a quick going-over for them.

Exit the **Burglar** *into the mezzanine bathroom.*

. . . to make his entrance.———

——— *Enter* **Vicki**, *holding the sardines and a white bathmat, and* **Roger**, *carrying the box and bag, from the downstairs bathroom.*

Frederick *takes over the search in* **Dotty**'s *clothes.*

Vicki   A *bathmat?*

Roger   Better than nothing!

Vicki   I can't go around in front of our taxpayers wearing a *bathmat!*

He leads the way upstairs.

Roger   *I'll* look in the bedroom. You look in the other bathroom.

—— *Exit* **Roger** *into the bedroom and* **Vicki** *into the mezzanine bathroom.*

Garry *makes his exit* ——— *and is amazed to see* **Dotty** *now apparently embracing* **Frederick.**

Garry *starts downstairs to attack* **Frederick.** *But he is still hobbled and in any case . . .*

Frederick *has to make his entrance.* ———————

—— *Enter* **Philip** *through the front door.*

Garry *tries to get* **Brooke** *to untie him.*

Philip   Darling! Help! Where are you?

But **Brooke** *blindly has to make her entrance.* ————

—— *Enter* **Vicki** *from the mezzanine bathroom.*

Lloyd *takes over the search of* **Dotty**'s *clothing.* **Garry** *gazes in astonishment.*

Vicki   Roger! Roger!

Tim *enters from the dressing-rooms and hands* **Lloyd** *a cactus.*

Exit **Philip** *hurriedly, unseen by* **Vicki**, *into the downstairs bathroom.*

Vicki   There's someone in the bathroom now!

Brooke *runs towards the bedrooms then stops.* **Belinda** *watches this anxiously.* ———

—— **Flavia** (*off*) Oh, darling, I'm finding such lovely things!

Lloyd *hands the cactus to* **Dotty** *without looking at it while he searches.*

Vicki *turns and runs downstairs instead, as* **Flavia** *enters along the upstairs corridor, absorbed in the china tea service she is carrying.*

Garry *hobbles downstairs, takes the cactus from the distracted* **Dotty**, *and rams it into* **Lloyd***'s bottom. Then he hobbles back upstairs, still holding the cactus.*

Lloyd *tries to pursue him . . .*

. . . but stops with a cry of pain.——————————

Vicki *exits hurriedly into the downstairs bathroom.*

Flavia   Do you remember this china tea service –

————— **Vicki** *screams, off.*

Flavia   – that you gave me on the very first anniversary of our . . . ?

Enter **Vicki** *from the downstairs bathroom. She stops at the sight of* **Flavia**.

Garry *puts the cactus down on the platform. He takes the ends of the black and white bedsheets that are hanging up outside the bedroom door, waiting for* **Frederick** *and* **Brooke**, *and ties them together.*

Flavia   Who are you?

Vicki   Oh *no* – it's his wife and dependents!

She puts her hands over her face.

Enter **Philip** *from the downstairs bathroom, still with his hands encumbered, holding the bathmat now as well, and keeping his trousers up with his elbows.*

Philip   Excuse me, I think you've dropped your dress.

Flavia *gasps.* **Philip** *looks up at the gallery and sees her.*

Philip (*to* **Flavia**)   Where have you been? I've been going mad! Look at the state I'm in!

He holds up his hands to show **Flavia** *the state he is in and his trousers fall down. The tea service slips from* **Flavia**'s *horrified hands, and rains down on the floor of the living-room below.* **Philip** *hurries towards the stairs, trousers round his ankles, his hands extended in supplication.*

Philip   Darling, honestly!

—— **Vicki** *flees before him, comes face to face with* **Flavia**, *and takes refuge in the linen cupboard.*

Philip   She just burst into the room and her dress fell off!

Exit **Flavia**, *with a cry of pain, along the upstairs corridor.*

—— *Enter* **Roger** *from the bedroom, directly in* **Philip**'s *path.*

Philip *holds up the bathmat in front of his face. He is invisible to* **Roger**, *though, because the latter is holding up a white bedsheet.*

Roger   Here, put this sheet on for the moment while I see if there's something in the attic.

Brooke *makes her exit* ——

Brooke *begins to take off her overcoat.*

Garry *picks up the cactus, but then has to hand it to* **Brooke**. *She peers at it, baffled, while . . .*

. . . **Garry** *makes his entrance.*————————

Brooke *comes down from the platform holding the cactus, then stops in amazement, overcoat half on and half off, at the sight of* **Lloyd** *lowering his trousers and* **Dotty** *pulling needles out of his bottom.*

Garry *makes his exit* ——
and also watches the scene below
in amazement. So does
Belinda.

—— Roger *leaves* Philip
with the sheet and exits along
upstairs corridor.

Philip *turns to go back*
downstairs.

Enter Burglar *from the*
mezzanine bathroom, holding two
gold taps.

Burglar   One pair gold
taps . . .

Garry *hobbles downstairs and*
takes the cactus from Brooke
for use against Lloyd *again.*

He stops at the sight of Philip.

Oh, my Gawd!

Philip   Who are you?

Burglar   Me? Fixing the
taps.

Tim *warns* Lloyd *about*
Garry.

Lloyd *quickly pulls up his*
trousers.

Philip   Tax? Income tax?

Burglar   That's right,
governor. In come new taps
. . . out go old taps.

Exit Burglar *into the*
mezzanine bathroom.

Tim *takes the cactus from*
Garry. Garry *snatches it*
back, then has to hand it back to
Tim *anyway so that he can grab*
Vicki'*s dress from its hook*
and . . .

Philip   Tax-inspectors
everywhere!

Roger *(off)*   Here you are!

Philip   The other one!

Exit Philip *into the bedroom,*
holding the bathmat in front of his
face.

. . . make his entrance. ———

Lloyd *lowers his trousers again for* **Dotty** *to resume operations.*

——— *Enter* **Roger** *along the upstairs corridor, holding* **Vicki***'s dress.*

Roger   I've found your dress! It came flying out of the attic at me!

——— *Exit* **Roger** *into mezzanine bathroom.*

Enter **Philip** *from the bedroom, trying to pull the bathmat off his head.*

Philip   Darling! I've got her dress stuck to my head now!

Enter **Roger** *from the mezzanine bathroom.*

Garry *makes his exit* ——— *and* **Lloyd** *hurriedly decides that he needs no further attention.*

——— *Exit* **Philip** *into the bedroom.*

Roger   Another intruder!

Enter the **Burglar** *from the mezzanine bathroom.*

Frederick *makes his exit* ——— *and picks up the bedsheets, which are waiting for him and* **Brooke** *to put on. He flaps them at* **Brooke** *to remind her about her change.*

Lloyd *points out the flapping sheets to her, but she puts the overcoat back on to storm out again.* **Lloyd** *detains her desperately while he takes the cactus from* **Tim** *and gives it to her as a token of his enduring affection. She peers at it and he takes in the nature of the present for the first time himself. He turns in pained query to* **Tim***, who gestures that it was all the shop*

Burglar   Just doing the taps, governor.

Roger   Attacks? Not attacks on women?

Burglar   Try anything, governor, but I'll do the taps on the bath first.

had left – all the rest of their stock is now on **Poppy**'s *desk.*

Lloyd *takes the cactus back and kisses it, with painful results, to present to* **Brooke** *again.* **Frederick** *flaps the sheets in desperation.*

Brooke *hesitates. Finally she takes off her overcoat, runs up the steps with the cactus.*

Selsdon *makes his exit.——* **Brooke** *pushes the cactus into* **Selsdon**'s *hands as she passes.*

There is a swirl of sheets as **Frederick** *attempts to dress* **Brooke** *in time for her entrance.*

Frederick *and* **Brooke** *make their separate entrances —— and discover that they are unable*

Exit **Burglar** *into the mezzanine bathroom.*

Roger   Sex maniacs everywhere! Where is Vicki? Vicki . . . ?

Exit **Roger** *into the downstairs bathroom.*

Enter **Burglar** *from the mezzanine bathroom, heading for the front door.*

Burglar   People everywhere! I'm off. A tax on women? I don't know, they'll put a tax on anything these days.

Enter **Roger** *from the downstairs bathroom. The* **Burglar** *stops.*

Roger   If I can't find her, you're going to be in trouble, you see.

Burglar   WC? I'll fix it.

—— *Exit* **Burglar** *into the mezzanine bathroom again.*

Roger   Vicki . . . ?

Exit **Roger** *through the front door.*

——**Philip** *attempts to enter from the bedroom.*

*to because their sheets are attached
to each other.*

Belinda, *upstairs for her
entrance, goes to disentangle them.
So does* **Selsdon**, *but he and
the cactus together makes things
worse.*

Frederick *and* **Brooke** *are
half on and half off.*——————   —— **Vicki** *attempts to enter*
Garry *watches with pleasure,*   *from the linen cupboard.*
until **Lloyd** *furiously drives
him . . .*

. . . on stage to hold the fort.——   —— *Enter* **Roger** *through the
front door.*

Garry improvises.——————   —— **Roger**   No Sheikh
yet! I thought he was coming
Tim *takes off his raincoat and*   at four? I mean, it's nearly,
starts to put on the spare sheet to   you know, four now . . .
go on as **Frederick**'s *double.*   Well, it's after three . . .
Lloyd *rips it off him again, and*   Because I've been standing
gestures that it's needed as an   here for a good, you know, it
emergency substitute for   seems like forever . . . What's
Frederick's *sheet. They pass*   the time now. It must be
the sheet to **Frederick**, *but he*   getting on for* five . . .
*is too entangled to do anything
with it.*

Belinda *gestures desperately to*
Lloyd *for the real* **Sheikh**'s
robes. **Lloyd** *passes them up to*
Belinda, *who hands them to*
Frederick . . .

. . . who is dragged on ————   —— Oh, you're here
through the linen cupboard door   already, hiding in the,
by **Brooke**, *still holding the*   anyway . . . And this is your
second sheet and the real   charming wife? So you want
Sheikh's *robes.*   to see over the house now,

Belinda *takes the cactus away from* **Selsdon**, *then hurriedly hands it down to* **Lloyd** *so that . . .*

. . . she can make her entrance. ————————————

Lloyd *puts the cactus in a safe place on the chairs downstairs.*

Tim *puts on the bathmat as burnous, to go on as* **Philip**'s *double, but gestures to* **Lloyd** *that he now has no sheet to wear, because it has vanished on stage with* **Frederick**.

They both register despair.

Lloyd *takes a despairing pull of whisky.*

do you, Sheikh? Right. Well. Since you're upstairs already

Roger *goes upstairs.*

———— *Enter* **Flavia** *along the upstairs corridor, carrying a vase.*

Flavia　Him and his floozie! I'll break this over their heads!

Roger, **Philip** *and* **Vicki** *go downstairs.*

Roger (*to* **Philip** *and* **Vicki**) I'm sorry about this. I don't know who she is. No connection with the house, I assure you.

Enter **Mrs Clackett** *from the service quarters, with another plate of sardines.* **Roger** *advances to introduce her.*

Mrs Clackett　No other hands, thank you, not in my sardines, 'cause this time I'm eating them.

Roger *ushers* **Philip** *and* **Vicki** *away from* **Mrs Clackett** *towards the mezzanine bathroom.*

He opens the door to the mezzanine bathroom.

Roger　But in here . . .

Flavia　*Arab* sheets?

Belinda *exits.* ——————

Lloyd *and* **Tim** *indicate the problem of the missing sheet to her.*

She instantly indicates **Tim**'s *own raincoat.*

Lloyd *puts it on* **Tim** *back to front.*

They both gloomily inspect the result.

Frederick *makes his exit* —— *dragging* **Brooke** *backwards with him, since they are still attached to each other.*

Selsdon *improvises a line.* ——

Brooke *struggles back on,* —— *as best she can.*

Tim *makes his entrance in back-to-front raincoat.* ——————

Frederick *has picked up the real burnous and flaps it in desperation as he realises that the*

—— *Exit* **Flavia** *into the bedroom.*

Roger   In here we have . . .

Enter the **Burglar** *from the mezzanine bathroom.*

Burglar   Ballcocks, governor. Your ballcocks have gone.

Roger   We have him.

Enter **Flavia** *from the bedroom.*

Mrs Clackett   You give me that sheet, you devil!

She seizes the nearest sheet and it comes away in her hand to reveal **Vicki**.

Flavia *comes downstairs menacingly.*

—— *Exit* **Philip** *discreetly into the study.*

—— **Burglar**   It's my little girl! So far as I could see before she went.

—— **Vicki**   Dad!

—— *Enter* **Philip** *from the study in amazement.* (*He is now played by a double –* **Tim**.)

robes are still somewhere on stage. All **Lloyd** *can find now as a substitute is* **Brooke**'s *leopard-skin overcoat. He spins* **Frederick** *round to put it on him back to front, as he did with* **Tim** *and the raincoat. He then crams the burnous on* **Frederick**'s *head, but* **Frederick** *has continued to turn, so it hangs over his face instead of his neck.* **Lloyd** *crams the* **Sheikh**'s *dark glasses on top of the burnous . . .*

. . . and **Frederick** *stumbles blindly back on stage.* ————

Lloyd *picks up the whisky, takes a weary swig, and is just about to sit down on the cactus when he springs up again guiltily, because* **Poppy** *is standing agitatedly in front of him.*

She takes the whisky away from him and puts it down, desperate to secure his full attention. She whispers urgently to him. He can't understand. She whispers again, becoming more and more agitated. He puts a hand to his ear, meaning he can't hear.

Burglar   Our little Vicki, that ran away from home, I thought I'd never see again!

Flavia (*threateningly*)   So where's my other sheet?

———— *Enter through the front door a* **Sheikh**, *played by* **Frederick**.

Sheikh   Ah! A house of heavenly peace! I rent it!

Roger   Hold on, hold on . . . I know that face! (*Pulls the* **Sheikh**'s *burnous aside to reveal his face.*) He isn't a sheikh! He's that sex-maniac!

They all fall upon him, and reveal that his trousers are around his ankles.

Burglar   And what you're up to with my little girl down there in Basingstoke I won't ask. But I'll tell you one thing, Vicki

Vicki   What's that, Dad?

Poppy (*screams to* **Lloyd** *in despair*) I'm going to have a . . .

Selsdon *flings the front door open.* ————————————

Selsdon   Good old-fashioned plate of *what* . . . ?

Poppy   . . . *baby*!

Selsdon *goes back on stage.* ——

Poppy *claps her hand over her mouth, horrified.*

Lloyd (*whispers*)   And curtain, perhaps?

Poppy   Oh . . . !

She runs back to the corner to bring the curtain down.————

Everyone appears in the doors and windows, eager to know more.

Lloyd *subsides, defeated, on to the cactus and springs up again in agony.*

CURTAIN

Burglar   When all around is strife and uncertainty, there's nothing like a . . .

—— *He dries and goes to the front door.*

————————

Selsdon   A good old-fashioned plate of gravy!

———————— CURTAIN

Act Three

The curtain goes up to reveal the tabs of the Municipal Theatre, Stockton-on-Tees. A half-empty whisky bottle nestles at the foot of them. The introductory music for Nothing On.

As the music finishes the tabs begin to rise. A foot or two above stage level they stop uncertainly, hover for a moment, and fall again.

Pause.

The introductory music starts again and is then faded out.

Enter **Tim** *from the wings, in his dinner jacket, but with elements of the* **Burglar***'s gear visible beneath it, and the* **Burglar***'s cap on his head.*

Tim   Good evening, ladies and gentlemen. (*He removes the* **Burglar***'s cap.*) Welcome to the the Old Fishmarket Theatre, Lowestoft, or rather the Municipal Theatre, Stockton-on-Tees, for this evening's performance of *Nothing On.* We apologise for the slight delay in starting tonight, which is due to circumstances . . .

Belinda (*off, screaming but indistinguishable*)   Hands off Freddie! All right?

Dotty (*off, screaming but indistinguishable*)   You're the one who's trying to get their hands on Freddie!

Tim   . . . due to circumstances . . .

Dotty (*off, screaming but indistinguishable*)   You don't own him, you know!

Tim   . . . beyond our control . . .

The sound of a slap, off, and **Dotty** *screams in pain, off.*

. . . and we would ask you to bear with us for a moment while we deal with her. With them. With the circumstances. I should perhaps say that with tonight's performance of the play our long and highly successful tour . . .

Poppy (*over Tannoy*)   Ladies and gentlemen. We apologise for the delay in starting tonight, which is due to circumstances which have . . .

Belinda (*over Tannoy*)   Don't you dare! Don't you dare!

Poppy (*over Tannoy*)   . . . which have now been brought under control.

Tim   . . . our long and highly successful tour is on its very last legs. Its very last leg. Thank you for your . . .

Poppy   Thank you for your . . .

Tim *and* **Poppy** (*together*)   . . . co-operation and understanding.

Tim   I sincerely trust . . .

He pauses for an instant to see if he will be interrupted again.

I sincerely trust there will be no other . . .

He becomes aware of the whisky bottle.

. . . no other hiccups. No other hold-ups. So, ladies and gentlemen, will you please sit back and enjoy the remains of the evening.

Exit **Tim**. *A slight pause, then his arm comes out from under the tabs and retrieves the bottle.*

The introductory music for Nothing On, *and this time the tabs rise. The act is being seen from the front again, exactly as it was the first time, at the rehearsal in Weston-super-Mare.*

Enter slowly and with dignity from the service quarters, limping painfully, **Mrs Clackett**. *She is holding a plate in her left hand and a handful of loose sardines in her right.*

Mrs Clackett (*bravely*)   It's no good you going on . . .

She stops and looks at the phone. It hurriedly starts to ring.

I can't pick sardines off the floor *and* answer the phone.

She dumps the handful of sardines on the plate.

I've only got one leg.

She shifts the plate to her right hand and picks up the phone with the left.

(*into the phone, bravely*)   Hello . . . Yes, but there's no one here . . . No, Mr Brent's not here . . .

She puts the plate of sardines down next to the newspaper on the sofa as she speaks and picks up the newspaper. She shakes the outer sheet free and wipes her oily hand on it as best she can. The rest of the newspaper disintegrates and falls back on top of the sardines.

He lives here, yes, but he don't live here now because he lives in Spain. Mr Philip Brent, that's right . . . The one who writes the plays, only why he wants to get mixed up in plays God only knows, he'd be safer off in the lion's cage at the zoo . . . No, she's in Spain, too, they're all in Spain, there's no one here . . . Am *I* in Spain . . . ?

She realises that she is holding the sheet of newspaper instead of the sardines. She turns round to look for them as she speaks, winding herself into the telephone cord.

No, I'm not in Spain, dear. I look after the house for them, but I go home at one o'clock on Wednesday, only I've got a nice plate of sardines to put my feet up with . . .

She sits down uncertainly on the heap of newspaper.

. . . because it's the royal what's it called on the telly – the royal you know . . .

She realises that she is sitting on the sardines and extracts the plate as discreetly as possible as she speaks.

. . . And if it's to do with letting the house then you'll have to ring the house agents, because they're the agents for the house . . . Squire, Squire, Hackham and who's the other one . . . ?

She examines the flattened contents of the plate.

No, they're not in Spain, they're just a bit squashed. Squire, Squire, Hackham and, hold on . . .

She stands up to go, uncertainly balancing plate, sheet of newspaper and phone.

. . . I'm going to do something wrong here.

She starts to go, then realises there are loose sheets of newspaper all over the floor and bends down to pick them up. The sardines slide off the plate on to the floor.

Always the same, isn't it.

She starts to go again.

One minute you've got too much on your plate . . .

She realises that she has nothing on her plate, turns round and sees the sardines.

. . . next thing you know they've gone again.

She uncertainly drops a few sheets of the newspaper over the sardines and exits into the study, holding the empty plate and the telephone receiver. The body of the phone falls off its table and follows her to the door

The sound of a key in the lock. The front door opens. On the doorstep is **Roger***, carrying a cardboard box.*

Roger   . . . I have a housekeeper, yes, but this is her afternoon off.

Enter **Vicki***.*

The body of the phone begins to creep inconspicuously towards the door.

Roger   So we've got the place entirely to ourselves.

Roger *goes back and brings in a flight bag and closes the front door.*

I'll just check.

He halts the telephone with a casually placed foot. **Vicki** *gazes round.*

Roger   Hello? Anyone at home? No, there's no one here.

He picks the phone up and puts it back on its table.

So what do you think?

He takes his hand off the phone and it springs back on to the floor.

Vicki   Great. And this is all yours?

The phone starts to creep away again. **Roger** *casually picks it up as he talks and puts it down on the sideboard.*

Roger   Just a little shack in the woods, really. Converted posset mill. Sixteenth-century.

Vicki   It must have cost a bomb.

Another jerk on the wire catapults the phone across the room. **Vicki** *pays no attention to it.*

Roger   Well, one has to have somewhere to entertain one's business associates. Someone on the phone now, by the look of it.

He picks the phone up and puts it back on the sideboard.

It's probably this, you know, this Arab saying he wants to come at four, so I mean I'll just have a word with him and . . .

He tries to pick up the receiver and finds that it's not there. As the conversation continues he follows the receiver cord along with his hand.

Vicki   Right, and I've got to get those files to our Basingstoke office by four.

Roger   Yes, we'll only just manage to pick it in. I mean, we'll only just fit it up. I mean . . .

Vicki   Right, then.

Roger   We won't bother to pull the champagne.

He pulls gently at the cord.

Vicki   All these doors!

Roger   Oh, only a handful, really. Study . . . Kitchen . . . and a self-contained service flat . . .

He tugs hard and the cord comes away without the receiver.

. . . for the receiver.

Vicki   Terrific. And which one's the . . . ?

Roger   What?

Vicki   You know . . .

Roger   The usual offices? Through here, through here.

He bundles up the phone and cable, and opens the downstairs bathroom door for her.

Vicki   Fantastic.

Exit **Vicki** *into the bathroom.* **Roger** *tosses the phone casually off after her.*

Enter **Mrs Clackett** *from the study, still walking with difficulty and holding the now cordless receiver.*

Mrs Clackett   I've lost the sardines again . . .

Mutual surprise. **Roger** *closes the door to the bathroom.*

Roger   I'm sorry. I thought there was no one here.

Mrs Clackett   I'm not here. (*She looks round for the phone, so that she can replace the receiver.*) I don't know where I am.

Roger   I'm from the agents.

Mrs Clackett   Lost the phone now.

Roger   Squire, Squire, Hackham and Dudley.

Mrs Clackett   Never lost a phone before.

Roger   I'm Tramplemain.

Mrs Clackett   I'll just put it up here, look, if anyone wants it. (*She puts the receiver on top of the television.*)

Roger Oh, right, thanks. No, I just dropped in to . . . go into a few things . . .

The bathroom door opens. **Roger** *closes it.* **Mrs Clackett** *gets down on her hands and knees, and looks under the newspaper.*

Roger Well, to check some of the measurements . . .

The bathroom door opens. **Roger** *closes it.* **Mrs Clackett** *goes to scoop up the sardines, but then looks round.*

Roger Do one or two odd jobs . . .

The bathroom door opens. **Roger** *closes it.*

Mrs Clackett Now the plate's gone.

Roger Oh, and a client. I'm showing a prospective client over the house.

The bathroom door opens.

Vicki What's wrong with this door?

Roger *closes it.*

Roger She's thinking of renting it. Her interest is definitely aroused.

Enter **Vicki** *from the bathroom.*

Vicki That's not the bedroom.

Roger The bedroom? No, that's the downstairs bathroom and WC suite. And this is the . . .

Roger *steps forward on to the newspapers to introduce* **Mrs Clackett**. *His foot slides away in front of him.*

Mrs Clackett Sardines, dear, sardines.

Vicki Oh. Hi.

Roger She's not really here.

Mrs Clackett (*looking under the newspaper*) Oh, you shouldn't have stood on them.

Roger (*to* **Mrs Clackett**)   Don't worry about us.

Mrs Clackett   They'll all go standing on them now.

Roger   We'll just inspect the house.

Mrs Clackett   I'd better give the floor a wash.

Exit **Mrs Clackett** *into the study, leaving the sardines beneath the newspaper on the floor.*

Roger   I'm sorry about this.

Vicki   That's all right. We don't want the television, do we?

Roger   Television? That's right, television, she didn't explain about wanting to watch this royal, you know, because obviously there's been this thing with the . . . (*He indicates the sardines.*) I mean, I'm just, you know, in case anyone's looking at all this and thinking, 'My God!'

Vicki   Great. Come on, then. (*She starts upstairs.*) I've got to be in Basingstoke by four.

Roger   Sorry, love. I thought we ought to get that straight.

Vicki   We'll take it up with us.

Roger   Where are we?

Vicki   And don't let my files out of sight.

Roger   Hold on. We've got out of . . .

Vicki   What?

Roger   What?

Vicki   Her?

Roger   Her? OK . . . 'her'. Right, because she *has* been in the family for generations.

Enter **Mrs Clackett** *from the study, carrying a fire-bucket and a mop.*

Mrs Clackett Sardines . . . Sardines . . . It's not for me to say, of course, dear, only I will just say this: don't think twice about it – take the plunge . . . (*She plunges the mop into the fire-bucket.*) You'll really enjoy it here . . . (*She discovers that the mop won't go into the fire-bucket.*)

Vicki Oh. Great.

Mrs Clackett *removes the obstruction – a bottle of whisky.*

Mrs Clackett I'll put it here, look, then if he wants it he won't know where to find it . . .

Mrs Clackett *puts the bottle of whisky with the other bottles on the sideboard.*

Vicki Terrific.

Mrs Clackett Sardines, sardines. (*She hands the mop to* **Roger**.) You'll have to do the sardines, then, 'cause I've got to go back to the kitchen now and do some more sardines.

Exit **Mrs Clackett** *to service quarters.*

Vicki You see? She thinks it's great. She's even making us sardines!

Roger (*contemplates the bucket and mop uncertainly*) Well . . .

Vicki I think she's terrific.

Roger Terrific.

Vicki So which way?

Roger I don't know – kind of parcel them up in the . . . (*He holds out some sheets of newspaper to her.*) And I'll . . . (*He demonstrates the mop.*)

Vicki (*starts up the stairs*) Up here?

Roger Down here!

Vicki In here?

Roger OK, *I'll* do the . . . *you* do the . . .

Exit **Vicki** *into the mezzanine bathroom.* **Roger** *parcels up the sardines in the newspaper as best he can.*

Vicki   It's another bathroom. (*She reappears.*)

Roger *dumps the parcel of sardines on the telephone table while he dabs hurriedly at the floor with the mop.*

Roger   Take the box upstairs, then! Take the bag!

Vicki   Always trying to get me into bathrooms.

Roger   Bag! Box!

Vicki *moves to stand outside the airing cupboard.*

Vicki   Oh, black sheets!

Roger (*runs to the stairs with bucket and mop, and holds them out to* **Vicki**)   All right, take the . . . take the . . . take the . . . !

Vicki   Oh, you're in a real state!

Roger (*despairingly*)   Oh . . . !

Roger *runs back and abandons the bucket and mop to pick up the bag and box.*

Vicki   You can't even get the door open.

Exit **Vicki** *into the bedroom.*

Roger *runs back to collect the bucket and mop, just as the front door opens to reveal* **Philip**, *carrying a cardboard box.*

Philip   No, it's Mrs Clackett's afternoon off, remember. We've got the place . . .

Philip *freezes, as* **Roger** *flees upstairs with the bag and the box.* **Philip** *follows* **Roger**'*s progress out of the corner of his eye.*

Enter **Flavia**, *carrying a flight bag like* **Roger**'*s.*

The bedroom door shuts in **Roger**'*s face. He opens the door again and exits into the bedroom with the bag and box.*

Philip   . . . entirely to ourselves.

Flavia   Home.

Philip   Home, sweet home.

Flavia   Dear old house!

Philip   Just waiting for us to come back!

Flavia (*producing the remains of the phone*)   But how odd to find the telephone in the garden!

Philip   I'll put it back.

She hands him the phone – now in a very deteriorated condition – and he attempts to replace it on the telephone table. But it is still connected to its lead, which is too short, since it runs out through the downstairs bathroom door and back in through the front door.

Flavia   I thought I'd better bring it in.

Philip   Very sensible. (*He tugs discreetly at the lead.*)

Flavia   Someone's bound to want it.

Philip   Oh dear. (*He tugs.*)

Flavia   Why don't you put it back on the table?

Philip   The wire seems to be caught.

Flavia   Oh, look, it's caught round the downstairs bathroom.

Philip   So it is.

Philip *takes the phone back out of the front room.* **Flavia** *with discreet violence pulls the lead out of the junction box where it originates.* **Philip** *re-emerges with the phone through the downstairs bathroom.*

Flavia   I think I've disentangled it.

Philip   I climbed through the bathroom window and . . . oh . . . oh . . .

He takes the parcel of sardines off the telephone table and puts the telephone in its place.

Flavia   It's rather funny, though, creeping in like this for our wedding anniversary!

Philip   It's damned serious! If Inland Revenue find out we're in the . . .

Attempting to fold up the newspaper tidily, he becomes distracted by the contents that come oozing out over his hands. His voice dies away.

Flavia   . . . country, even for one night . . .

Philip   Sorry. (*He puts down the parcel of sardines on the sofa.*) Yes, because if Inland Revenue find out we're in the . . .

He moves towards the champagne and slides, exactly like **Garry**, *on the oily patch on the floor. He stops and looks back on it in surprise.*

Flavia   . . . country . . .

Philip (*distracted*)   . . . country . . .

Flavia   . . . even for one night.

Philip   . . . even for one night. . .

Philip *edges cautiously away from the oily patch.*

Flavia   . . . bang goes . . .

He bangs into the bucket and mop.

Flavia   . . . our claim to be resident abroad . . .

Philip *fumbles for his handkerchief and claps it to his nose.*

Philip   Resident abroad. Absolutely. (*He looks into his handkerchief.*)

Flavia   Bang goes most of this year's income.

Philip   Most of this year's income . . . (*He puts the handkerchief away.*) So, yes, I think I'd better . . . (*He picks up bag and box, clutches them to himself for reassurance.*) . . . go and have a little lie-down.

He starts up the stairs.

Flavia (*surprised, but rallying*)   Lie-down, yes, well, why not? No children. No friends dropping in . . . (*She moves the sofa to cover the oily patch as she speaks.*) We're absolutely on our . . . Leave those!

Philip   Oh, yes.

Philip *puts the bag and box down, but by this time he is already upstairs.*

Flavia   Downstairs! Not upstairs!

Philip   I'm so sorry. I . . . (*He looks in his handkerchief again.*) Oh dear . . .

He exits hurriedly into bedroom.

Flavia (*picks up the fire-bucket and mop*)   There is something to be said for being a tax exile . . . (*She flees upstairs with the fire-bucket and mop, laughing.*) Sh . . . ! What? Inland Revenue may hear us!

Enter **Mrs Clackett** *from the service quarters carrying a fresh plate of sardines.*

Mrs Clackett (*to herself*)   What I did with that first lot of sardines I shall never know.

She puts down the plate of sardines, and goes to sit on the sofa, on the parcel of sardines left there by **Philip**.

Flavia (*urgently, looking down from the gallery, still holding the bucket and mop*)   Mrs *Newspaper*!

Mrs Clackett *jumps up.*

Mrs Clackett   Oh, you give me a turn! My heart jumped right out of the sofa!

Flavia   So did mine! We thought you'd gone!

Mrs Clackett (*finding the parcel of sardines and examining it*)   I thought you was in Sardinia!

Flavia   We are! We are! You haven't seen us! We're not here!

Mrs Clackett   I can guess which one of them put this here.

Flavia   Yes, but the main thing is that the Income Tax are after us.

Mrs Clackett   Lovely helping of sardines to sit on.

Flavia   So if anybody asks for us, you don't know nothing. Anything. So I'll just . . . I'll just . . . get a hot-water bottle.

She goes towards the mezzanine bathroom.

Mrs Clackett   And off she goes without waiting to find out about his letters.

Flavia (*stops, realises despairingly*)   His letters?

Enter **Philip** *groggily from the bedroom.*

Philip   Letters? What letters? You forward all the mail, don't you?

Mrs Clackett   Not presents from Sardinia, dear.

Philip   I'm so sorry.

Exit **Philip** *into the bedroom.*

Mrs Clackett   I'll show you where I put presents from Sardinia.

She goes upstairs towards **Flavia**, *who is still outside the mezzanine bathroom, carrying the bucket and mop, not sure which way to move.*

I put presents from Sardinia in the pigeonhouse.

Flavia   In the *pigeonhouse?*

Mrs Clackett   In the little pigeonhouse down here, love.

She stuffs the parcel of sardines down the front of **Flavia**'s *dress.* **Flavia** *looks down at the dress, then at the fire-bucket and mop she is carrying.* **Mrs Clackett** *retires hurriedly back downstairs and exits into the study, with* **Flavia** *after her.*

Enter **Roger** *from the bedroom, still dressed, but with no tie on.*

Roger   Yes, but I could hear voices!

He falls over **Philip**'s *bag and box.*

Enter **Vicki** *from the bedroom in her underwear.*

Vicki   Voices? What sort of voices?

Roger   Box voices. I mean, *people*'s boxes.

Vicki   But there's no one here.

Roger   Darling, I saw the door-handle move! And these bags . . . I'm not sure they were, you know, when we went into the, do you know what I mean?

Vicki   I still don't see why you've got to put your tie on to look.

Roger (*picking up the bag and box*)   Because if someone left these things outside the, I mean, come on, they obviously want them downstairs inside the, you know.

Vicki   Mrs Clockett?

Roger   It could be. Coming up here on her way to, well, carrying various, I mean, who knows?

Vicki (*looking over the banisters*)   Oh look, she's opened our sardines.

She moves to go downstairs. **Roger** *puts down the bag and box outside the linen cupboard and grabs her.*

Roger   Come back!

Vicki   What?

Roger   I'll fetch them! You can't go downstairs like that.

Vicki   Why not?

Roger   Mrs Crackett.

Vicki   Mrs Crackett?

Roger   One has certain obligations.

Enter **Mrs Clackett** *from the study, fishing sardines out of the front of her dress.*

Mrs Clackett (*to herself*)   Sardines here. Sardines there. It's like the Battle of Waterloo out there.

Roger *tries to pull open the linen cupboard door to conceal* **Vicki**, *but it is obstructed by the bag and box.*

Mrs Clackett   Oh, you're still poking around, are you?

Roger   Yes, still poking, well, still pulling.

He tugs at the door again, unaware of the obstruction, and the handle comes off as it opens.

Mrs Clackett   Good job I can't see far with this leg.

Roger *moves the bag and box, gets* **Vicki** *inside the linen cupboard and rebalances the handle in place.*

Roger   Just, you know, trying all the doors and I mean checking all the door handles.

He starts downstairs, carrying **Philip**'s *bag and box.*

Mrs Blackett.

Mrs Clackett   Clackett, dear, Clackett.

Roger   Mrs Clackett. Is there anyone else in the house, Mrs Clackett?

Mrs Clackett   I haven't seen no one, dear.

Roger   I thought I heard a box. I mean, I found these voices.

Mrs Clackett   Voices? There's no voices here, love.

Roger   I must have imagined it.

Philip (*off*)   Oh, good Lord above!

The colossal sound of **Philip** *falling downstairs, off, taking half the platform with him, followed by a wailing groan.*

Roger   I beg your pardon?

Mrs Clackett (*mimicking* **Philip**)   Oh, good Lord above!

She crashes things about on the sideboard in imitation of the off-stage crash and ends the performance with a wailing groan.

Roger   Why, what is it?

Mrs Clackett   The study door's open.

She crosses and closes the door.

Roger   They're going to want these inside the . . . (*He indicates the study.*) So I'll put them outside the . . . (*He indicates the front door.*) Then they can, do you know what I mean?

Exit **Roger** *through the front door, carrying the bag and box.*

Enter **Flavia** *from the mezzanine bathroom, carrying a first-aid box. She sees the linen cupboard door swinging open as she passes, and pushes it shut, so that the latch closes. The handle comes off in her hand.*

Flavia   Nothing but flapping doors in this handle.

Exit **Flavia** *into the bedroom, holding the first-aid box and the handle. Enter from the study* **Philip**, *holding a tax demand and its envelope. The part is now being played not by* **Frederick** *but by* **Tim**.

Philip/Tim   . . . final notice . . . steps will be taken . . . distraint . . . proceedings in court . . .

Mrs Clackett   Oh, my Lord, who are you?

Philip/Tim   I'm Philip.

Mrs Clackett   You're Philip? What happened to you?

Philip/Tim   Well, it's all got a bit slippery on the stairs out there.

Mrs Clackett   You haven't done himself an injury?

Philip/Tim   No. He's just a bit shaken. I'll be all right in a minute.

Exit **Mrs Clackett** *to the study.*

Philip/Tim   You weren't going to tell me a gentleman had come about the house, were you?

Mrs Clackett (*off*)   What?

Philip/Tim   You weren't going to tell me a gentleman had come about the house?

Enter **Mrs Clackett** *from the study.*

Mrs Clackett   That's right. A gentleman come about the house.

Philip/Tim   Don't tell me. I'm not here.

Mrs Clackett   Oh, and he's put your box out in the garden for you.

Philip/Tim   Let them do anything. Just so long as you don't tell anyone we're here.

Mrs Clackett   So I'll just sit down and turn on the . . . sardines, I've forgotten the sardines! (*She finds the second plate of sardines on the table, exactly where she put it.*) Oh, no, I haven't – I've remembered the sardines! What a surprise! I must go out to the kitchen and make another plate of sardines to celebrate.

Exit **Mrs Clackett** *to the service quarters.*

Philip/Tim   I didn't get this! I'm not here. I'm in Spain. But if I didn't get it I didn't open it.

Enter **Flavia** *from the bedroom. She is holding the dress that* **Vicki** *arrived in and the handle of the linen cupboard.*

Flavia   Darling . . . (*She stares at* **Philip/Tim** *in surprise, then recovers herself and looks at the dress.*) *I* never had a handle like this, did I?

Philip/Tim (*abstracted*)   Didn't you?

Flavia   I shouldn't buy anything as brassy as this.

Flavia *drops the dress and attempts to replace the handle on the linen cupboard behind her back.*

Oh, it's not something you gave me, is it?

Philip/Tim   I should never have touched it.

Flavia   No, it's lovely.

Philip/Tim   Stick it down. Put it back. Never saw it.

Exit **Philip/Tim** *into study.*

Flavia   Well, I'll put it in the attic, if anyone else wants to have a try.

Exit **Flavia** *along the upstairs corridor, taking the handle but leaving the dress on the floor.*

Enter **Roger** *through the front door, without the bag and box.*

Roger   All right, all right . . . Now the study door's open again! What's going on?

He goes towards the study, and opens and closes the door. He reacts to the sound of urgent knocking overhead.

Knocking.

Knocking.

Upstairs!

He runs upstairs. Knocking.

Oh my God, there's something in the . . . (*He discovers the lack of a handle.*) Oh my God! (*Knocking.*) Listen! I can't, because the handle has, you know. You'll just have to . . .

He demonstrates pushing. Knocking.

Come on! Come on!

Knocking.

I mean, whatever it is in there. Can you hear me? Darling!

Knocking.

Look, don't just keep banging! There's nothing I can, I mean it won't, there's nowhere to . . .

Knocking. He opens the bedroom door.

Listen! Climb round into the . . . (*He indicates the bedroom*)
Squeeze through the, you know, and shin down the, I mean,
there must be *some* way!

Knocking.

Oh, for pity's sake!

Exit **Roger** *into the bedroom.*

Enter **Philip** *from the study, holding a tax demand and an envelope.
He is now being played by* **Frederick**, *with a plaster on his head.*

Philip   '. . . final notice . . . steps will be taken . . . distraint
. . . proceedings in court . . .'

Enter **Roger** *from the bedroom, pulling* **Vicki** *after him.* **Philip**
gazes at them, baffled.

Roger   Oh, it's you.

Vicki   Of course it's me! You put me in here! In the dark
with all black sheets and things.

Roger   I put you in *there*, but you managed to squeeze
through the, you know.

Vicki   Why did *I* lock the door? Why did *you* lock the
door!

Roger   I couldn't, I mean, look, look, it's come off!

Vicki   *Someone* locked the door!

Philip   Sorry.

Exit **Philip** *apologetically into study.*

Roger   Anyway, we can't stand here like this.

Vicki   Like what?

Roger   I mean, you know, with people going in and out.

Vicki   OK, I'll take it off.

Roger   In here, in here!

He ushers her into the bedroom.

Enter **Philip** *cautiously from the study, holding the tax demand and the envelope.*

Philip   '. . . final notice . . . steps will be taken . . . distraint . . . proceedings in court . . .'

Enter **Roger** *from the bedroom, holding the first-aid box.*

He looks up and down the landing.

Enter **Vicki** *from the bedroom.*

Philip *stares at them.*

Vicki   Now what?

Roger   A hot-water box! *I* didn't put it there!

Vicki   *I* didn't put it there.

Philip   Sorry.

Exit **Philip** *into the study.*

Roger   Someone in the bathroom, filling first-aid bottles.

Exit **Roger** *into the mezzanine bathroom.*

Vicki (*anxious*)   You don't think there's something creepy going on?

Exit **Vicki** *into the mezzanine bathroom.*

Enter **Flavia** *along the upstairs corridor.*

Flavia   Darling . . . Darling?

Enter **Philip** *cautiously from the study. He raises the income tax demand to speak.*

Flavia   Darling, are you coming to bed or aren't you?

Exit **Flavia** *into the bedroom.*

Philip *raises his income tax demand to speak.*

Enter **Roger** *and* **Vicki** *from the mezzanine bathroom.*

Roger   What did you say?

Vicki   I didn't say anything.

Exit **Philip** *into the study.*

Roger   I mean, first there's the door handle. Now there's the first water box.

Vicki   I can feel goose pimples all over.

Roger   Yes, quick, get something round you.

Vicki   Get the covers over our heads.

Roger *is about to open the bedroom door.*

Roger   Just a moment. What did I do with those sardines?

He goes downstairs. **Vicki** *makes to follow.*

Roger   You – wait here.

Vicki (*uneasily*)   You hear all sorts of funny things about these old houses.

Roger   Yes, but this one has been extensively modernised throughout. I can't see how anything creepy would survive oil-fired central heating and . . .

Vicki   What? What is it?

Roger *looks round.*

Vicki   What's happening?

Roger   The sardines. They've gone. (*He double-takes on them.*) No, they haven't. They're here. Oh. Well. My God . . . I mean . . . my God!

He turns and starts back upstairs.

Flavia *crawls through the front door. She picks up the sardines and takes them back to the front door.*

Roger   You put a plate of sardines down for two minutes, and the last thing you expect to find, I mean, these days, the one thing you don't expect to find when you come back is a plate of, I mean that's *really* weird!

Vicki   Perhaps there is something funny going on. I'm going to get into bed and put my head under the . . .

She freezes at the sight of the empty table outside the bedroom door.

Roger   Because, I mean, there they are! Exactly where I . . .

He realises that the sardines are not there.

Vicki   Bag . . .

Roger *goes back downstairs to investigate.* **Vicki** *runs after him.* **Flavia**, *unseen by* **Roger**, *hesitates. She glances up towards the landing, reminded by the mention of the bag that she has failed to set it. She looks back at the table, realising that* **Roger** *now expects the sardines to be on the table.*

Roger   No, they're not. I suppose Mrs Sprockett must have, I mean, what *is* going on?

He looks at **Vicki**. **Flavia** *hurriedly replaces the sardines.*

Vicki   Bag!

Flavia *exits hurriedly through the front door.*

Roger   Bag?

Vicki   Bag! Bag!

She drags **Roger** *back upstairs.*

Roger   What do you mean, bag, bag?

Roger *looks over the banisters and sees the sardines.*

Sardines!

Vicki   Bag! Bag! Bag!

Roger   Sardines! Sardines!

Vicki   Bag! Bag! Bag!

Roger   Sardines! Sardines!

Vicki   Bag! Bag! Bag!

While **Roger** *is gazing at the sardines, and* **Vicki** *is looking at* **Roger**, *the bedroom door opens and* **Flavia** *puts the flight bag on the table outside.*

Roger (*tearing himsetf away from the sight of the sardines*)   Bag? What bag?

Vicki (*gazing at the bag*)   No bag!

Roger   No bag?

Vicki   Your bag! Suddenly! Here! Now – gone!

Roger   It's in the bedroom. (*He sees the bag.*) It was in the bedroom. I put it in the bedroom. I'll put it back in the bedroom.

As **Roger** *goes to open the bedroom door it opens in front of him, and* **Flavia** *begins to come out, carrying the box.*

Vicki   Don't go in there!

Roger *finds himself holding the box, with the door closing in his face.*

Roger   The box!

Vicki   The box?

Roger   They've *both* not gone!

Vicki   Oh! My files!

Roger   What on earth is happening? Where's Mrs Spratchett?

He starts downstairs with the bag and box. **Vicki** *follows him.*

Roger   You wait in the bedroom.

Vicki   No! No! No!

She runs downstairs.

Roger   At least put your dress on!

Vicki   I'm not going in there!

Roger   I'll fetch it for you, I'll fetch it for you!

He puts the bag and box down at the head of the stairs, returns to the bedroom and sees the dress on the floor.

Exit **Roger** *into the bedroom.*

Vicki   Yes, quick – let's get out of here!

Enter **Roger** *from the bedroom.*

Roger   Your dress has gone.

As he speaks he slides the dress over the edge of the gallery with his foot to get rid of it. It falls on top of **Vicki** *beneath and makes her jerk her head. She feels blindly around her; her lenses have gone again.*

Vicki   I'm never going to see Basingstoke again!

Roger   Don't panic! Don't panic! There's some perfectly rational explanation for all this.

He starts downstairs, looking over the banisters, appalled at the sight of **Vicki** *below, and falls headlong over the bag and box at the top of the stairs.*

Vicki *searches blindly behind the sofa for her missing lenses.*

Enter **Philip** *from the study. He is holding the tax demand and the envelope.*

Philip   . . . final notice . . . steps will be taken . . . distraint . . .

His voice dies away at the sight of **Roger** *lying at the bottom of the stairs.*

Enter **Flavia** *along the upstairs corridor, carrying various pieces of bric-a-brac.*

Flavia   Darling, if we're not going to bed I'm going to clear out the attic . . .

Philip (*to Roger*)   Oh dear. (*He claps a handkerchief to his nose.*)

Flavia   Oh, great heavens!

She rushes downstairs.

Enter **Mrs Clackett** *from the service quarters, holding another plate of sardines.*

Mrs Clackett   No other hands, thank you, not in my sardines . . . (*She sees* **Roger**.) . . . 'cause this time she has, she's gone and killed him!

Flavia   He's stunned, that's all. Keep going.

Roger (*lifting his head*)   Don't panic! Don't panic!

Flavia   He's all right! Just keep going!

Roger   There's some perfectly rational explanation for all this.

Mrs Clackett   Where are we?

Roger   I'll fetch Mrs Splotchett and she'll tell us what's happening . . .

Mrs Clackett   You've fetched her. I'm here.

Roger   I've fetched Mrs Splotchett and she'll tell us what's happening.

Mrs Clackett   She won't, you know.

Flavia   *I'll* tell you what's happening.

Roger   There's a man in there! Yes?

Flavia   He's not in there, my precious – he's in here, look, and so am I.

Mrs Clackett   No, no, there's no one in the house, love. Yes?

Flavia   No, look, I know this is a great surprise for everyone. I mean, it's quite a shock for us, finding a man lying at the bottom of the stairs! (*To* **Philip**.) Isn't it, darling?

Philip   Oh dear. (*He looks into his handkerchief.*) Oh dear, oh dear. (*He sits down hurriedly.*)

Flavia   But now we've all met we'll just have to . . . Well, we'll just have to introduce ourselves! Won't we, darling?

Philip   Introduce ourselves. (*He struggles to his feet, but has to sit down again.*) I'm so sorry.

Flavia   This is my husband. I'm afraid surprises go straight to his nose!

Vicki *rises blindly from behind sofa at her cue.*

Vicki   There's a man lurking in the undergrowth!

Flavia   Oh, how delightful – another unexpected guest. (*To* **Vicki**.) So why don't you . . . why don't you . . . see what you can see in the garden?

She pushes **Vicki** *out of the front door, and helps* **Philip** *to his feet.*

(*to* **Philip**)   And darling, you go off and get that bottle marked poison in the downstairs loo. That eats through anything.

Philip (*from behind his handkerchief*)   Eats through anything. Right. Thank you. Thank you. Yes, I've heard of people getting stuck with a problem, but this is ridiculous.

He opens the downstairs bathroom door to go off. A pane of glass drops out of the mullioned window, and an arm comes through and releases the catch. The window opens, and through it appears the **Burglar**, *played by* **Tim**.

Burglar/Tim   No bars. No burglar alarms. They ought to be prosecuted for incitement.

He climbs in and looks round in surprise to find the room full of people.

Mrs Clackett   Come in and join the party, love.

Flavia   A burglar! This is most exciting!

Philip   Oh dear, this is my fault. Because when I say, 'I've heard of people getting stuck with a problem, this is ridiculous', and I open this door. . .

He opens the downstairs bathroom again. Another pane of glass drops out of the mullioned window, and an arm comes through.

Enter through the window the **Burglar**, *played by* **Selsdon**.

Burglar/Selsdon   No bars. No burglar alarms. They ought to be prosecuted for incitement.

He climbs in, becoming uneasily aware of the others as he does so.

Burglar/Tim   No, but sometimes it makes me want to sit down and weep.

Mrs Clackett   I know, love, it's getting like a funeral in here.

Burglar/Selsdon   When I think I used to do banks!

Flavia   Just keep going.

Burglar/Selsdon *and* **Burglar/Tim** (*together*)   When I remember I used to do bullion vaults! What am I doing now? I'm breaking into paper bags . . .

Flavia   Keep going.

Burglar/Selsdon   Stop?

Flavia   No, no!

Burglar/Selsdon   I thought the coast was clear, you see. I saw him going out to the bathroom.

Flavia (closing the downstairs bathroom door)   Yes, never mind, it's all right. We'll think of something.

Burglar/Selsdon   Oh, no, I was listening most carefully. What's it he says?

Philip   'I've heard of people getting stuck with a problem, but this is ridiculous.'

Burglar/Selsdon   And he opened the door . . .

Burglar/Selsdon *opens the downstairs bathroom door to demonstrate.*

A third pane of glass drops out of the mullioned window, and an arm comes through. Enter through the window the **Burglar***, played by* **Lloyd***.*

Burglar/Lloyd   No bars. No burglar alarms. They ought to be prosecuted for incitement.

He climbs in, very uncertain what's happening to him. He doesn't know whether to react to the presence of the others or not.

Mrs Clackett   They always come in threes, don't they.

All Three Burglars   When I think I used to do banks! When I remember I used to do bullion vaults . . .

Flavia   Hold on! We know this man! He's not a burglar!

She snatches **Lloyd***'s* **Burglar** *hat off.*

He's our social worker!

Roger   He's *what?*

Flavia   He's that nice man who comes in and tells us *what to do*!

Lloyd (*appalled, faintly*)   What to do?

Others (*firmly*)   What to do!

Lloyd *is paralysed with stage-fright. He looks round helplessly and makes vague and ineffectual gestures.*

Selsdon   What's he saying?

Flavia   He's saying, he's saying – just get through it for doors and sardines! Yes? That's what it's all about! Doors and sardines! (*To* **Lloyd***.*) Yes?

Lloyd (*helplessly*)   Doors and sardines!

Others   Doors and sardines!

They all try to put this into practice. **Philip** *picks up the sardines and runs around trying to find some application for them. The others open various doors, fetch further plates of sardines, and run helplessly around with them.* **Lloyd** *stands helplessly watching the chaos he has created swirl around him.*

Flavia   He's saying, he's saying – 'Phones and police'!

Lloyd   Phones and police . . .

Philip   Phone!

Philip *and* **Roger** *are each handed a half of the phone.*

Roger   Police!

Roger *puts the receiver to his ear.* **Philip** *dials.*

Flavia   He's saying 'Bags and boxes'.

Others   Bags and boxes!

Everyone runs around with the two boxes and the two bags, all helplessly colliding with each other and running into the furniture.

Flavia (*decisively*)   Sheets, sheets! He's saying 'Sheets'!

Lloyd   Sheets . . .

Others (*desperately*)   Sheets!

Roger *runs out of the study door,* **Tim** *out of the front door.*

Flavia   He's saying 'All we want now is a nice happy ending!'

Roger *comes back at once propelling the helpless* **Vicki**, *wrapping her in the white sheet as they go.* **Tim** *comes back simultaneously with* **Poppy**, *cramming her into the real* **Sheikh**'s *robes.*

Dotty (*looking at* **Poppy**)   And here she is! In her wedding dress!

Flavia (*looking at* **Vicki**)   Yes, yes – it's their wedding day!

Mrs Clackett (*still looking at* **Poppy**)   It's their wedding day!

Others   Ah!

Flavia   What a happy ending!

Mrs Clackett *pushes* **Poppy** *to* **Lloyd***'s side.* **Flavia** *pushes* **Vicki** *to his other side.*

Mrs Clackett   Do you take this sheet to be your lawful wedded wife? If not, speak now, or forever hold your peace.

Lloyd *nods helplessly.*

Selsdon   What's he saying, what's he saying?

Flavia   He's saying . . . he's saying . . . 'Last line!'

Selsdon   Last line? Me?

All   Last line, last line!

Selsdon   When all around is strife and uncertainty, there's nothing like a good old-fashioned plate of . . .

He dries.

All (*holding up plates of sardines; beseechingly*)   Curtain!

Tableau. Then **Tim** *runs hurriedly off.*

CURTAIN

Except that it jams just above the level of their heads. As one man they seize hold of it and drag it down. A ripping sound. The curtain detaches itself from its fixings and falls on top of them all, leaving a floundering mass of bodies on stage.

Nothing On

Extracts from the programme

Grand Theatre

WESTON-SUPER-MARE

Proprietors: GRAND THEATRE (Weston-super-Mare) LIMITED
General Manager: E.E.A. GRADSHAW

The Grand Theatre Weston-super-Mare is a Member of the
Grand Group.

Evenings at 7.45
Matinee: Wednesday at 2.30
Saturday at 5.00
and 8.30

Commencing Tuesday 15th January for One Week Only

Otstar Productions Ltd
present

DOTTY OTLEY

BELINDA BLAIR
GARRY LEJEUNE

in

NOTHING ON

by

ROBIN HOUSEMONGER

with

SELSDON MOWBRAY
BROOKE ASHTON
FREDERICK FELLOWES

Directed by LLOYD DALLAS
Designed by GINA BOXHALL
Lighting by ROD WRAY
Costumes by PATSY HEMMING

WORLD PREMIERE PRIOR TO NATIONAL TOUR!

SMOKING IS NOT PERMITTED IN THE AUDITORIUM
The use of cameras and tape recorders is forbidden.
The management reserve the right to refuse admission, also to make any alteration in
the cast which may be rendered necessary by illness or other unavoidable causes.
From the theatre rules 'All exits shall be available for use during all performances'.
'The fire curtain shall be lowered during each performance'.

NOTHING ON

by ROBIN HOUSEMONGER

Cast in order of appearance:

Mrs Clackett	DOTTY OTLEY
Roger Tramplemain	GARRY LEJEUNE
Vicki	BROOKE ASHTON
Philip Brent	FREDERICK FELLOWES
Flavia Brent	BELINDA BLAIR
Burglar	SELSDON MOWBRAY
Sheikh	FREDERICK FELLOWES

The action takes place in the living-room of the Brents' country home, on a Wednesday afternoon.

for OTSTAR PRODUCTIONS LTD

Company and Stage Manager TIM ALLGOOD
Assistant Stage Manager POPPY NORTON-TAYLOR

Production credits
Sardines by Old Salt Sardines. Antique silverware and cardboard boxes by Mrs J.G.H. Norton-Taylor. Stethoscope and hospital trolley by Severn Surgical Supplies. Straitjacket by Kumfy Restraints Ltd. Coffins by G. Ashforth and Sons.

We gratefully acknowledge the generous support of EUROPEAN BREWERIES in sponsoring this production.

Behind The Dressing Room Doors

DOTTY OTLEY (Mrs Clackett) makes a welcome return to the stage to create the role of Mrs Clackett after playing Mrs Hackett, Britain's most famous lollipop lady ('Ooh, I can't 'ardly 'old me lolly up!') in over 320 episodes of TV's ON THE ZEBRAS. Her many stage appearances include her critically acclaimed portrayal of Fru Såckett, the comic char in Strindberg's SCENES FROM THE CHARNELHOUSE. Her first appearance ever? In a school production of HENRY IV PART I – as the old bag-lady, Mrs Duckett.

BELINDA BLAIR (Flavia Brent) has been on the stage since the age of four, when she made her debut in SINBAD THE SAILOR at the old Croydon Hippodrome as one of Miss Toni Tanner's Ten Tapping Tots. She subsequently danced her way round this country, Southern Africa, and the Far East in shows like ZIPPEDY-DOODA! and HERE COME LES GIRLS! More recently she has been seen in such comedy hits as DON'T MR DUDDLE!, WHO'S BEEN SLEEPING IN MY BED?, and TWICE TWO IS SEX. She is married to scriptwriter Terry Wough, who has contributed lead-in material to most of TV's chat shows. They have two sons and three retrievers.

GARRY LEJEUNE (Roger Tramplemain) while still at drama school won the coveted Laetitia Daintyman Medal for Violence. His television work includes POLICE!, CRIME SQUAD, SWAT, FORENSIC, and THE NICK, but he is probably best-known as 'Cornetto', the ice-cream salesman who stirs the hearts of all the lollipop ladies in ON THE ZEBRAS.

SELSDON MOWBRAY (Burglar) first 'trod the boards' at the age of 12 – playing Lucius in a touring production of JULIUS CAESAR, with his father, the great Chelmsford Mowbray, in the lead. Since then he has served in various local reps, and claims to have appeared with every company to have toured Shakespeare in the past half-century, working his way up through the Mustard-seeds and the various Boys and Sons of, to the Balthazars, Benvolios, and Le Beaus; then the Slenders, Lennoxes, Trinculos, Snouts, and Froths; and graduating to the Scroops, Poloniuses, and Aguecheeks. His most recent film appearance was as Outraged Pensioner in GREEN WILLIES.

BROOKE ASHTON (Vicki) is probably best known as the girl wearing nothing but 'good, honest, natural froth' in the Hauptbahnhofbrau lager commercial. Her television appearances range from Girl at Infants' School in ON THE ZEBRAS to Girl in Massage Parlour in ON PROBATION. Cinemagoers saw her in THE GIRL IN ROOM 14, where she played the Girl in Room 312.

FREDERICK FELLOWES (Philip Brent) has appeared in many popular television series, including CALLING CASUALTY, CARDIAC ARREST!, OUT-PATIENTS, and IN-PATIENTS. On stage he was most recently seen in the controversial all-male version of THE TROJAN WOMEN. He is happily married, and lives near Crawley, where his wife breeds pedigree dogs. 'If she ever leaves me,' he says, 'it will probably be for an Irish wolfhound!'

ROBIN HOUSEMONGER (Author) was born in Worcester Park, Surrey, into a family 'unremarkable in every way except for an aunt with red hair who used to sing all the high twiddly bits from THE MERRY WIDOW over the tea-table'. He claims to have been the world's most unsuccessful gents hosiery wholesaler, and began writing 'to fill the long hours between one hosiery order and the next'. He turned this experience into his very first play, SOCKS BEFORE MARRIAGE, which ran in the West End for nine years. Two of his subsequent plays, BRIEFS ENCOUNTER and HANKY PANKY, broke box office records in Perth, Western Australia. NOTHING ON is his seventeenth play.

LLOYD DALLAS (Director) 'read English at Cambridge, and stagecraft at the local benefits office'. He has directed plays in most parts of Britain, winning the South of Scotland Critics' Circle Special Award in 1969. In 1972 he directed a highly successful season for the National Theatre of Sri Lanka. In recent years he has probably become best known for his brilliant series of 'Shakespeare in Summer' productions in the parks of the inner London boroughs.

A Glimpse of the Noumenal

(condensed from J G Stillwater, *Eros Untrousered*
– Studies in the Semantics of Bedroom Farce)

The cultural importance of the so-called 'bedroom farce', or
'English sex farce', has long been recognised, but attention has
tended to centre on the metaphysical significance of mistaken
identity and upon the social criticism implicit in the form's
ground-breaking exploration of cross-dressing and trans-gender
role-playing. The focus of scholarly interest, however, is now
beginning to shift to the recurrence of certain mythic themes in
the genre, and to their religious and spiritual implications.

In a typical bedroom farce, a man and a woman come to some
secret or mysterious place (cf. *Beauty and the Beast, Bluebeard's Castle*,
etc.) to perform certain acts which are supposed to remain concealed from the eyes of the world. This is plainly a variant of the
traditional 'search' or 'quest', the goal of which, though presented
as being 'sexual' in nature, is to be understood as a metaphor of
enlightenment and transcendence. Some partial disrobing may
occur, to suggest perhaps a preliminary stripping away of worldly
illusions, but total nudity (perfect truth) and complete 'carnal
knowledge' (i.e. spiritual understanding) are perpetually fore-
stalled by the intervention of coincidental encounters (often with
other seekers engaged in parallel 'quests'), which bear a striking
resemblance to the trials undergone by postulants in various eso-
teric cults (cf. *The Magic Flute, Star Wars*, etc.).

A recurring and highly significant feature of the genre is a mul-
tiplicity of doors. If we regard the world on this side of the doors
as the physical one in which mortal men are condemned to live,
then the world or worlds concealed behind them may be thought
of as representing both the higher and more spiritual plane into
which the postulants hope to escape, and the underworld from
which at any moment demons may leap out to tempt or punish.
When the doors do open, it is often with great suddeness and
unexpectedness, highly suggestive of those epiphanic moments of
insight and enlightenment which give access to the 'other', and
offer us a fleeting glimpse of the noumenal.

Another recurring feature is the fall or loss of trousers. This can
be readily recognised as an allusion to the Fall of Man and the loss

of primal innocence. The removal of the trousers traditionally reveals a pair of striped underpants, in which we recognise both the stripes of the tiger, the feral beast that lurks in all of us beneath the civilised exterior suggested by the lost trousers, and perhaps also a premonitory representation of the stripes caused by the whipping which was formerly the traditional punishment for fornication.

Farce, interestingly, is popularly categorised as 'funny'. It is true that the form often involves 'funny' elements in the sense of the strange or uncanny, such as supposedly supernatural phenomena, and behaviour suggestive of demonic possession. But the meaning of 'funny' here is probably also intended to include its secondary sense, 'provocative of laughter.'

This is an interesting perception. It scarcely needs to be said that laughter, involving as it does the loss of self-control and the spasmodic release of breath, a vital bodily fluid, is a metaphorical representation of the sexual act. But it can also occasion the shedding of tears, which suggests that it may in addition be a sublimated form of mourning. Indeed we recognise here a symbolic foretaste of death. If sneezing has been widely feared because it is thought that during a sneeze the soul flies out of the body, and may not be recaptured (whence 'Bless you!' or '*Gesundheit!*'), then how much more dangerous is laughter. Not once but over and over again the repeated muscular contractions and expulsions of breath drive the 'soul' forth from the body. The danger of laughter is recognised in such expressions as 'killingly funny,' and 'I almost died'. There is a lurking fear that even more spectacular violence may ensue, and that a farce may end with a bloodletting as gruesome as in *Oedipus* or *Medea*, if people are induced to 'split their sides' or 'laugh their heads off'.

Fear of the darker undertones of bedroom farce has sometimes in the past led to its dismissal as 'mere entertainment'. As the foregoing hopefully makes clear, though, financial support by the Arts Council or a private sponsor for the tour of a bedroom farce would be by no means out of place.